"Building something that can last a lifetime is never a bad idea..."

Lilah laughed, the sound sweet and melodious. "I'm not so sure she's thinking about me and my wants and needs."

Noah nodded. "You have cultivated a nice backyard here. I can see why your daughter Sara wants to get married out among the roses and palm trees."

"She loves the wisteria and jasmine, and the old magnolias. That's why she picked May as the month for her wedding."

"Your jasmine will look pretty growing around a white gazebo. Like a wedding cake, for certain sure."

Lilah gave him a steady, unyielding stare. "You make it sound so romantic. Is this the part where you pitch the sale, Noah?"

He chuckled. "*Neh*, this is the part where I convince you to trust me. I can build you a near-perfect gazebo, but building trust requires a different kind of skill." He leaned toward her, his rocking chair squeaking. "A softer skill."

Lilah Mehl gazed into his eyes and waited for a beat or two. Then she let out a soft sigh and turned to face him again.

"When can you start?"

With over seventy books published and millions in print, **Lenora Worth** writes award-winning romance and romantic suspense. Three of her books finaled in the ACFW Carol Awards, and her Love Inspired Suspense novel *Body of Evidence* became a *New York Times* bestseller. Her novella in *Mistletoe Kisses* made her a *USA TODAY* bestselling author. Lenora goes on adventures with her retired husband, Don, and enjoys reading, baking and shopping...especially shoe shopping.

Books by Lenora Worth

Love Inspired

Pinecraft Seasons

Pinecraft Refuge
The Widow's Unexpected Suitor

Amish Seasons

Their Amish Reunion
Seeking Refuge
Secrets in an Amish Garden

Men of Millbrook Lake

Lakeside Hero
Lakeside Sweetheart
Her Lakeside Family

Texas Hearts

A Certain Hope
A Perfect Love
A Leap of Faith

Visit the Author Profile page at LoveInspired.com for more titles.

The Widow's Unexpected Suitor

LENORA WORTH

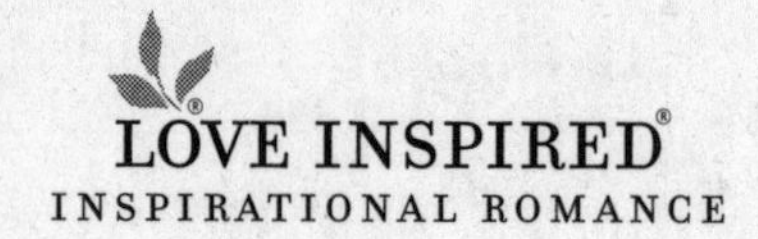

PLEASE RECYCLE · THIS PRODUCT IS RECYCLABLE

Recycling programs for this product may not exist in your area.

ISBN-13: 978-1-335-59882-0

The Widow's Unexpected Suitor

For questions and comments about the quality of this book, please contact us at CustomerService@Harlequin.com.

Love Inspired
22 Adelaide St. West, 41st Floor
Toronto, Ontario M5H 4E3, Canada
www.LoveInspired.com

Printed in Lithuania

Before they call, I will answer;
and while they are yet speaking, I will hear.
—*Isaiah* 65:24

Dedicated in memory of Patsy Thompson,
an avid reader and prayer warrior.
I miss your letters, Miss Patsy!

Chapter One

"A gazebo?"

Lilah Mehl stared at her eldest daughter, Sara, and wondered what the bride-to-be would request next. The wedding was only a few weeks away and now Sara had come up with yet another far-fetched idea. And one that would cost a bit of money at that.

"In the back garden, Mamm," Sara said, her burnished hair shimmering against her white organza *kapp*. She looked out toward the big back yard. "White and bright and we'll put sheers draped with flowers all the way around the top. Won't that be lovely?"

"So lovely," sixteen-year-old Carol said in a dreamy drawl, her big brown eyes wide with interest. "And we can enjoy it after the wedding. We can have frolics there, and it will come in handy on church days, too."

Thirteen-year-old Dana bobbed her head. She had hazel eyes, a mixture from both sides of the family, that were now vivid with curiosity. "I'd love that. I can sit there and read or visit with friends. It would be so pretty in the corner of the yard, Mamm." Slanting her head, she gave Lilah a grin. "You've been thinking about how to make that spot look more welcoming."

Lilah had a flash of a memory from long ago. Her husband, Joshua, had laughed when she'd told him she wanted to make this backyard a sanctuary. "I reckon I'll have to build you a gazebo or some type of potting shed out there."

"I'd love that," she'd replied, thinking that might take a while. Now he was gone, but she'd worked on her garden to keep her grief at bay. Talking about a gazebo only brought that grief back.

"Mamm?" Sara gave her a quizzical stare, as if she wanted to say something more.

"I see you've all been discussing this," Lilah said, a long sigh following her words. She sank down on a chair in the kitchen of their small cottage, the sound of gulls cawing off in the distance reminding her that summer was coming to Pinecraft and so was this wedding. She wasn't ready for either.

"We've tried to work out the details," Sara said, pulling out her wedding journal. "I have drawn up a plan, and I've found pictures in magazines. I have some money saved, and I can contribute to the cost. I'm sure Abram will, too."

"Abram has to take care of you the rest of his life," Lilah reminded her beautiful daughter. "Don't go asking for his money just yet. I have a little left, but honestly, I'm not sure how much more our budget can be stretched."

Sara's pout told Lilah this discussion wasn't over. But for now, it had to be. Lilah had cut corners and gathered willing friends to help make everything from placemats to dresses for her girls. She'd worked in the garden all spring and sold plants to bring in money. People all over the neighborhood came to her for gardening advice and to buy budding plants and vegetables. But she was afraid to call in any more favors.

"Let's get supper going and we'll discuss this later," she told her daughters. "At least we're finished the dresses, and your lovely colors of mint for your sister, and pink for your attendants will be so pretty with all the flowers blossoming in the yard."

"That's the plan," Sara replied, clutching her worn wedding journal tightly to her chest. She'd been planning her wedding since she was twelve, and now that it was real she'd been adding to her plans almost every day for months now.

Lilah had to blink back tears. She wished her

Joshua could be here to see this but he'd died a decade ago after having heart trouble all his life. He'd loved his three girls so much.

"Mamm," Sara said, wrapping her arms around her mother's shoulders. "I'll figure out a way. The gazebo will be pretty for the wedding, but you can sit there and enjoy it after I'm gone. It will have a nice roof so you won't have to sit in the sun. I thought it might help you… once I'm married and out of the house."

Lilah touched a hand to Sara's arm. "Sometimes, you surprise me, you know that? Are you being sincere or just trying to butter me up?"

Sara sat down beside her while Carol and Dana pulled out cold chicken, sliced fresh vegetables and dinnerware. "Mamm, I'm serious. I've told you Abram works for a man who builds houses, but this man also creates beautiful gazebos and pergolas."

Lilah didn't recall who Abram worked for, but he had a great job that paid well and that's all that mattered. "I don't know, Sara. I'll have to think about this."

Sara quieted for a moment, that hint of hesitation making Lilah wonder what she was really up to. "After I saw a gazebo photo in a magazine, Abram suggested you'd need something pretty once I move out."

"She has something pretty," Carol called out. "My sister and me. You're not the favorite."

"You are all my favorite," Lilah said, thinking she would miss Sara. But she'd have more time to focus on her younger daughters. She'd neglected them lately during all this wedding planning, but not on purpose. Still, they might think that.

Shaking her head, she smiled at her eldest. "This idea is a sweet sentiment, Sara, but we still have much to do over the next three weeks."

Then they heard a knock at the door.

Sara's green eyes widened. "I...uh... I might have asked the man to come over and take some measurements and such."

"Sara?" Lilah stood and straightened her apron. "What man? What have you done?"

"She invited Noah Lantz over here to build you a gazebo, Mamm," Dana blurted out with an elaborate shrug, her *kapp* crooked as usual.

"Noah Lantz?" Lilah shook her head. "I know of him and I'm telling all of you, he's too busy building cottages and tiny homes for tourists to help us out. Why would he want to build a gazebo in my backyard?"

"He's the man Abram works for," Sara replied. "I know I've mentioned him before."

"Not by name," Lilah said. "Abram doesn't talk about his new job very much, but I imagine

Noah Lantz has to be too busy to stop and build something in my yard, wedding or no wedding."

"Let's hear him out and see what he says," Sara replied as she hurried to the door.

Lilah didn't know whether to laugh or cry. Had she spoiled her girls to the point that they'd ignore her motherly concerns? This wedding and its demands had become a wake-up call for her, making her wonder why she was just now seeing things clearly.

When the door opened, she stood still and firm, her back ramrod straight, and took in the sight of a man she'd only seen on billboards. He was tall, muscular and had thick salt-and-pepper hair and a nice smile. His eyes were a deep blue that startled her. But she ignored all of that and got right to the point.

"I'm so sorry you came here this late, but there must be a misunderstanding," she said, waving him into the small sitting room. "You can't possibly have time to build a gazebo in the yard before my determined daughter's wedding. So thank you anyway and *gut* night."

Noah Lantz started chuckling, which made him look more approachable and normal, but it only added to her surprise and anger.

He gave her an endearing glance. "Is that how you greet guests who come to your home?"

"*Neh*," she said, her spine stiffening even

more. "My girls just informed me of this ridiculous plan to hire someone to build this gazebo thing in time for a wedding that is less than a month away. Who does that?"

"I do," he said, his tone gentle and full of an amused sparkle. "I'd love to build a gazebo for you, Lilah Mehl. That is, if you'll let me." He grinned and held his hands on his suspenders. "Because right now, it looks as if you'd rather bite nails than let me enter your home."

Lilah stepped back. "I'm so sorry. Where are my manners? We can talk, *ja*. But we were just about to eat supper." A moment went by before she did the proper thing. "You could stay and join us if you'd like."

Sara let out a gasp, her eyes blazing with fire. "I had not planned on this."

Lilah gave her a motherly stare. "I had not planned on hiring someone to do work we don't need and pay them with money I don't have. He will stay for supper."

Noah's deep blue eyes widened in appreciation. "That sure does sound *gut*, but I must admit I've never had a supper invitation worded in quite that way. I accept. *Denke*."

Lilah could feel the heat of a flush on her face. She motioned him into the small dining room, while her eldest daughter glared at her as if she'd burned their food. "Mamm, he doesn't need to stay for supper."

"You heard me," Lilah replied in a whisper. "I can't be rude. You didn't tell me you'd already invited him here, so you'll just have to get over whatever you're feeling right now. He will have a meal with us while we talk about your gazebo idea. Unless you want to be the one to tell him to leave."

Sara let out a huff of breath. "This isn't going the way I'd thought it would go."

Lilah smiled and touched her daughter's arm. "That's for certain sure. Not what I'd planned either. Use your manners and remember the lesson you've learned tonight."

Noah Lantz entered the dining room, his presence making the room shrink. He looked larger than life, the same as he looked on the billboards advertising his housing company. He had dark hair with a touch of gray at the temples, but he looked as healthy as a horse to her. Lilah patted her own golden-brown hair and hoped her gray wasn't showing.

Don't be vain.

"Do you need to wash up?" she asked to hide the flurry of tingling nerves cascading against her skin. What was wrong with her?

"I'll show you the washroom," Carol offered, clearly intrigued by all this. "It's right this way."

Noah went into the small washroom, but quickly came back to the dining area, his deep gaze taking in the driftwood gray table and chairs and Lilah's love of fresh flowers. Did he find her cottage lacking?

Turning to Lilah, he said, "It's nice to meet you. I've seen you at church but never had the opportunity to speak to you. When Abram told me you were to be his mother-in-law, I was surprised. He and Sara really want to make the gazebo happen. I hope you'll hear me out regarding this project."

"I'll hear you out," she replied, her tone sweet and kind, her mind racing as she tried to remember seeing him at the church up the street that the Mennonites shared with the Amish. "But I don't need a gazebo in my yard."

Noah nodded. "If you say so. I sure am hungry."

He went to help the girls pour tea while Lilah stood there, her heart hammering a new tune, her mind opening to things she'd shut down years ago.

He was a nice man. A nice widowed man, from what she'd heard. They did have that in common, at least.

Noah hadn't expected to eat supper with Lilah and her curious daughters, but now that he was here enjoying thick slices of cold chicken, he realized he missed this—being with others at the end of the day, laughing and joking, telling the latest news or gossip. Sharing.

He missed sharing his life with someone special. His wife, Janeen, had always filled his days with laughter and fellowship. She'd forced him to go to many a frolic or singing just to get him out of the house. She loved walks in the park because she could watch the children playing there. She loved people, loved chatter and discussions and festivals. He didn't care so much for other people—at least not being with them. She'd called him an introvert.

A person who is comfortable being by himself.

Only now, he hated being by himself.

"Is the food that bad?" Dana asked, her gaze studying him as if he were a bullfrog.

Noah snapped to attention. "*Neh*, the food is *wunderbar gut*," he admitted. "I was just remembering."

"Your wife." Lilah's statement hit him with a soft wave of grief that crashed through his heart with a pounding velocity.

He nodded. "I don't get out much."

Sara glanced from Noah to her *mamm*. "Do you have friends?"

"Sara!"

Noah held up his hand. "I do have friends, *ja*. Your Abram and I have become *gut* friends. But I'm the quiet type. I am comfortable without a lot of people around." He took a sip of his sweet tea with lemon. "I miss my Janeen at times such as this."

Dana gave him another long stare. "You mean, you don't like eating supper alone, ain't so?"

"Dana!" Lilah shot her blunt daughter a warning stare, then shot him an embarrassed, apologetic look. "I'm sorry. I have taught them manners but they are curious."

"Your daughters are smart," he said to Lilah. Too smart. He'd need to remember that and watch *his* manners around this little cottage full of women.

"They are indeed," Lilah replied. "Let's take our dessert and go out onto the back porch. Just you and me, so we can talk in private about this gazebo."

"I want to hear," Sara said, her tone as sharp as a kitchen knife. "I have ideas."

"Me, too," Carol replied, her words more cautious.

Dana bobbed her head. "*Ja*, lots of ideas I'm guessing." She was having fun.

"*Neh*," Lilah replied, her gaze on Sara. "You sprung this…idea on me so now I need to hear the facts—how much will it cost and do I have that kind of money? Do we need a gazebo for the wedding? Do I want construction going on in my yard for the next few weeks?"

"I need to be in on that," Sara said, giving her mother an intense glance. "I'm the bride."

"I'm the one who'll decide about the gazebo," Lilah replied, her tone as firm as a two-by-four piece of lumber.

Noah held his amused smile behind what he hoped was a solemn expression. But suddenly he missed being a *daed*, too. More than he'd realized. Why was it so hot in this little kitchen and dining room? He felt a trickle of sweat shivering down his spine.

"Girls, bring the *kaffe* and key lime pie out to the porch—just ours, please. You three can have your pie after you've done the dishes."

Sara gave her *mamm* a long, complicated stare that held so many emotions, Noah didn't even want to unpack it. Abram Troyer had warned Noah about the Mehl women. But Abram's *daed* and Noah went back a long way. He was mostly doing this as a favor and a wedding present. Well, a present that could keep on giving after the wedding. Lilah Mehl looked as if she belonged in a gazebo, her hair so prim and proper even when the waning sun hit it and turned it to gold, and her polite manners once she'd decided he'd be having dinner with them, so refreshing and sweet.

Whoa. He needed to do the job and keep on moving. His heart would never go through another loss again. Never.

He remembered Abram's words regarding the Mehl girls.

"Tough, stubborn and a bit spoiled. But their *mamm*, Lilah, is the salt of the earth."

He followed Lilah out onto the deep back porch. "This is a nice place to enjoy the evening."

She smiled. "My Joshua bought us this house the first time we came down to Pinecraft. Back then, houses here were not that expensive and he loved the warm sunshine and the ocean air. We worked hard to renovate it. Then when his heart got so bad, we sold our farm and moved here permanently. He was supposed to rest and get better but he loved working with the local farmers. We had several good years together before his weak heart just gave out."

Noah studied the sturdy porch posts and the solid white railings. "He built this porch?"

She nodded. "Now my daughter thinks I need a gazebo to distract me after she leaves. Joshua mentioned projects he wanted to complete, but he never got to them. Sara is a lot like her *daed*, always dreaming up things she plans to do, but not always following through."

He smiled at that. "I don't think she liked you asking me to supper."

"She doesn't like most of what I decide, but she shouldn't react so strongly about supper since she invited you here without my knowledge."

"It is kind of her to think of you, though. Wanting to build something that can last a lifetime is never a bad idea."

Lilah laughed, the sound as sweet and melodious as the butterfly wind chimes hanging at the end of the porch. "I'm not so sure she's thinking completely about me and my wants and needs."

Noah nodded and stared out at the garden. "You have cultivated a nice backyard here. I can see why Sara wants to get married out amongst the roses and palm trees."

"She loves the wisteria and jasmine and the old magnolias. That's why she picked May as the month for her wedding."

"Your jasmine will look pretty growing around a white gazebo. Like a wedding cake, for certain sure."

Lilah gave him a steady, unyielding stare. "You make it sound so romantic. Is this the part where you pitch the sale, Noah?"

He chuckled. “*Neh*, Lilah, this is the part where I convince you to trust me. I can build you a near-perfect gazebo, but building trust requires a different kind of skill.” He leaned toward her, his rocking chair squeaking. “A softer skill.”

Lilah Mehl stared into his eyes and waited for a beat or two before she looked out into the gloaming. Then she let out a soft sigh and turned to face him again. “When can you start?”

Chapter Two

Two days later, Noah studied Lilah Mehl's backyard and jotted thoughts and ideas in his pocket notebook. The morning dew sparkled like lost diamonds across the lush green grass. A hibiscus bush bloomed a bright smiling pink next to the porch, while the queen palms and palmetto bushes swayed to music only they could hear through the balmy breeze.

He'd done his homework, asking around about the Mehls. Apparently, Lilah didn't just love her garden. She grew plants to sell, and he'd heard that everyone, from her neighbors and tourists to the fancy *Englisch* who lived over on the bay, came here each spring to buy the tiny containers of flowers and plants she'd nursed and nurtured in a small greenhouse at the far end of the long backyard. She also had a small foursquare vegetable garden on the sunnier side of the yard, neat and clean the way everything about her home and yard appeared.

She'd mentioned that she made a nice living from this garden. A pretty, pristine gazebo could add to the charm. She had told him she liked butterflies, too. She had walking stones covered with butterfly motifs and several butterfly-shaped chimes, along with several plants and citrus trees that attracted butterflies.

"They are a nuisance to some because they can destroy the citrus plants, but they are also beautiful when they emerge from their cocoons. All part of nature's plan."

He made note of that, several ideas in his head now. Thankful for the ideas, Noah knew *Gott* had a hand in him getting this job. He'd been going down that black hole of grief, regret and remorse again. It always came on suddenly, and without provocation, but these last few weeks of hard work and clients wanting things right now had almost made him want to retire from construction and building homes that needed to withstand a hurricane. That he didn't mind. He wanted his homes to be safe. But some customers were just determined to not be happy, he'd decided.

This one shouldn't have that problem. Lilah seemed like a calm, level-headed but loving woman. And she wasn't hard to look at either. Pretty and fresh-faced, with a lovely heart-shaped face and big, curious green eyes. She was a proper woman, for certain sure.

The garden had a purpose. She'd created pebbled and shell-covered walkways that flowed like an open maze all over the yard. The colors of the earth popped out at him while he walked the perimeter and marveled at her green thumb. Everything from jasmine and morning glory vines to roses and sunflowers gave this garden a feeling of welcomeness and peace and a bit of whimsy.

"What do you think?"

Noah whirled to find her standing there wearing a green dress and floral flip-flops, her *kapp* white and clean, her eyes as green as the lush grass underneath their feet. She wasn't too tall, but she wasn't tiny either. She was just right, he decided.

He wanted to tell her he thought she looked as pretty as her big yard. Then he quickly also decided he needed to concentrate on the task at hand. "I think you have worked hard to make this one of the most beautiful places in Pinecraft."

She moved toward him, her body like a willow tree swaying in the wind. "It started after Joshua got sick. I came out here to take my mind off of his illness and, well, to rant a bit to the Lord. I have to admit I did most of the talking and *Gott* did most of the listening."

Noah knew that feeling well. "They say we're closer to *Gott* in a garden."

"I think so," she replied. "I don't know exactly when it happened, but I began to rant less and pray more. That calmed me down and I was able to accept that my husband was dying." She lifted a hand toward her yard. "I began to see the blessing in this big yard I used to complain about. When the butterflies and birds gather here, it makes me happy." She shrugged. "Joshua was the one who encouraged me to create my dream garden. As if he knew..."

Noah's heart filled with a bouquet of emotions that choked at him like clinging vines. "But it still stays with you, ain't so? The grief?"

Lilah nodded, her chin tilted toward the colors exploding around them. "Every day. You would know."

Noah moved a little closer. "I do know. My grief is still fresh and new and it sometimes takes my breath away. I try to avoid people, so these side jobs are my way of working through my feelings."

Her eyes flared at that admission. "I see. You have a *gut* excuse to escape a big worksite then?"

"I do, and this one especially is a treat. I'm ready to get going. What have you decided?"

She took another tentative step. "First, I won't bother you while you work. Nor will the girls. Second, I will trust your judgment and let you figure out the best design. Third, not too fancy. I can only pay what I have. You never did name your fee."

Noah tugged at his straw hat. "I'll know that total when I finish the job. Depends on the materials, my labor and whether or not you like it, but I can promise it will be affordable."

She laughed and his heart chimed like the tiny bells she had on the garden gates. "Well, then I might just not like it. You can't tear it down, but if I hate it I don't have to pay, right?"

"You got me there," he said, grinning. "Smart woman. But I think you'll probably like it enough that I can get *kaffe* money."

She glanced back at the house. "You can get *kaffe* here for free if you do a *gut* job."

Noah liked that idea. "Got me again. Let me do some measuring and speculating and I'll be ready for that *kaffe*."

"I made a pound cake if you'd like a piece."

He chuckled and looked out over the petunias and lilies she'd placed around an old crape myrtle tree. "This project is getting better and better."

She smiled, nodded and left like a scared doe. He knew she'd meant it when she'd said she wouldn't bother him. He'd have to gain her trust and frankly, she'd have to gain his, too. He'd given up a lot after his wife died. Hadn't wanted to work or eat—or live, for that matter. But the bishop reminded him of *Gott*'s will. Noah had to accept that Janeen wasn't here in the flesh, but she was for certain sure here in spirit.

The bishop had told him, "She would want you to carry on and have a life of purpose, Noah. Do your work and know that Janeen would be proud. That can be a comfort when the grief tries to take you down."

Gott knew best. Noah didn't want to accept that, but what else could he do? It was part of his faith. Some days were just worse than others.

But *Gott* had always provided. *Gott* showed Noah which way to go each and every day. Today, he liked the direction he seemed to be going. He liked it here in this secret garden tucked away behind the dainty light blue cottage with the long front porch and the secluded back porch. Surrounded by old live oaks and towering pines, it seemed far away from the hurrying pace of the city.

He liked Lilah and her inquisitive, chatty daughters, too. Not used to lively conversation, he'd enjoyed soaking it up at supper the other night.

Only, he wasn't ready to like anyone. He wanted to wallow a bit more in his misery and wonder why Janeen had to die, why they'd never had children to carry on the family name. He'd wandered around as he'd wondered, and *Gott* had given him a lot of answers. Some that he didn't like, and others that made perfect sense.

Building this gazebo did make perfect sense. A wedding in a garden, a gazebo to remember the happy day and a spot to make new memories beyond the marriage ceremony. He could do this. He could make Lilah and her girls a lovely structure to complement a lovely garden.

But could he do it and risk losing his heart again? That was the question. He had to be overreacting about how Lilah made him feel. She'd fed him and she'd been polite and kind to him. That was all. He was just a lonely man who hadn't ventured out much other than to work. He hadn't thought of another woman since Janeen had taken her last breath. Why was he acting like a schoolboy with his first crush? He couldn't do that, wasn't ready to be that kind of man.

He'd get this done quickly because the wedding was only weeks away and because he didn't want to linger much in this inviting, enticing garden. It would be mighty hard to leave each day, knowing he'd go home to a lonely, stark house.

Noah focused on his measurements and then he sat down on an old wrought-iron chair and wrote down his thoughts and made a primitive sketch of what he saw in his head. Would Lilah like his design?

An hour later, she appeared on the porch with a percolator, two cups, cream and sugar, and a big slice of pound cake. After lowering the round tray down onto a bistro table, she waved to him.

"Would you rather eat alone?"

Noah should have said yes to that question. But he couldn't. "*Neh*," he called. "I want to show you my plans for the gazebo."

She nodded, but when he reached the porch, she held up a hand. "I think I'd like to be surprised. I need something to think about and if you show me the plan, I'll know how it will look. Let me see it when it's finished."

Noah had never met a woman like Lilah. "But you'll see it going up every day."

She thought about that. "You're right. You can't hide it from me. I can sit and watch it being built, see a new surprise each day, but the finished product will still be exciting."

"I suppose I could cover it every night then."

"*Neh.* That would be silly. I'd just go and peek anyway."

He took off his hat and went to the faucet by the steps and washed up. "I had a feeling you wouldn't be able to resist and I think you watching and checking on me will be the highlight of my days working here."

She looked confused, and then she blushed and motioned to a rocking chair, but she kept her head down as she poured the *kaffe* and passed him the cream and sugar, which he declined.

Noah looked into her eyes when she finished. "I like it black and strong."

"Then you'll enjoy this cupful."

Noah had no doubt he'd enjoy the brew and the cake and the company. He wouldn't make any more suggestive remarks because he wanted Lilah to feel comfortable around him. He wanted her to like him, too.

But he'd regret that later when he returned home and the memories greeted him like fluttering caught butterflies, making him want to give up all over again.

"Mamm, why were you out there on the porch with Noah Lantz?"

Lilah turned to find Sara standing in the living room, her hands on her hips in that familiar way that meant she was displeased. She'd done that even as a toddler. Put her tiny hands on her little hips and demanded attention. It was cute then, but annoying now.

"I offered the man some cake and *kaffe*."

"You don't need to feed him," Sara said, her brow furrowed. "He's hired to do a job."

Lilah didn't like Sara's mixed signals. Sara might be selfish at times, but she had always been polite to visitors. "Daughter, you are not to tell me what I can and can't do. I know you have wedding jitters, but you are the one who wanted a gazebo at the last minute. Why are you being so rude now?"

Sara blinked away the furrowed brow and let out a sigh. "I'm sorry, Mamm. I'm tired. I worked a full day at the Beachside Café and Albert got mad because I gave a customer two doughnuts instead of one. I had to pay for the one I gave away."

"That's disturbing," Lilah said. She heard stories of Albert Kempton, the manager of the new café, from Sara almost every day. "I suppose the man does like to make a profit. Did you give the customer an extra one on purpose?"

"*Neh*," Sara said as she hurried to the kitchen sink to wash her hands. "I mean I did hear the customer tell his wife he wasn't hungry and she could have the doughnut. Then I saw him searching his pockets for change."

Lilah let out a chuckle. "You are ever surprising, my Sara. That was kind of you, but you did pay for the doughnut so that should appease Albert the Alligator."

They both started laughing at the nickname Sara had given her ornery boss. His wife Alicia had a nickname, too, and she was a sweet person so Sara called her Alicia the Awesome.

"We can't keep calling him that," Lilah whispered. "We don't use those kind of descriptions and you could be fired."

"I hope to quit once I'm married," Sara said, still glancing out to where Noah was measuring and putting down stakes to mark off the spot he'd chalked out for the gazebo. "Abram made *gut* money delivering for Dawson's Department Store. He's almost paid off the loan on the used truck he bought. Tanner told him Noah was looking for hardworking men and suggested he should apply. Noah offered him a higher salary since he's already familiar with construction." She shrugged. "And he can still deliver for Tanner on his off-days."

Tanner Dawson owned and operated the growing store, along with his sweet wife, Eva, who'd recently given birth to a fine little boy named Thomas. Tanner's daughter Becky was a preteen now. They had a thriving business and a strong marriage.

Lilah wanted that for her daughters.

"Abram works hard," Lilah said regarding the new job, hoping Sara would see that and do her part. "Your salary can help pay for the remodeling work on your cute little house."

Sara whirled around, a frown marring her oval face. "So you think I need to keep working?"

"For a while maybe," Lilah said. "But it's your life, and something you and Abram should discuss."

Sara nodded at that. "I'd rather be home with a pretty, clean house and maybe a *bobbeli* on the way."

Lilah started washing dishes. "All in good time, daughter."

Sara stared out the window again. "Noah helped Abram with our house, you know. He gave Abram some extra wood and tiles so we could finish the washroom and he had leftover paint that we put in our bedroom. A pretty light blue—like the sky."

"I'll have to go back by there and see the progress." Lilah glanced at Noah, not surprised at him making a kind gesture. The man was muscular and strong, his shoulders broad and his arms tanned from the sun. Apparently, he had a big heart, too. "You never mentioned that or who exactly Abram works for with his new job. I'm surprised you didn't at least tell me."

Sara lifted her chin, then slanted her head. "We'd just become officially engaged when he first interviewed with Noah and my mind went into planning the wedding. I didn't know who Noah Lantz was then." She studied him out the window. "But I sure do now."

"You don't seem to want him here now, Sara. Are you sure you don't have something else to tell me? Did you hear something about Noah that displeased you?"

"*Neh*," Sara said. "I didn't mention him before because he wasn't on my mind until Abram suggested him for the gazebo," Sara admitted. "They only see each other in passing since Noah moves from one subdivision to the next just about every day, but they've become *gut* friends. He is a kind man, but he's still grieving his wife. Abram said they were very close."

"I'd hope so, since they were married."

Sara turned and folded some dish towels Lilah had brought in from the clothesline next to the washroom. "I mean a deep, abiding love, Mamm. The kind that's hard to shake."

"I loved your father that way," Lilah replied, wondering what Sara was really trying to say. She could always tell when her children were keeping things from her. But before they could get any further in this discussion, Carol and Dana came crashing through the house, followed by several friends.

Ah, summer. Always a chaotic, busy time but with the wedding even more so. Normally, an Amish wedding up North would take place in the fall or winter after the harvest was over, but here the Amish had weddings mostly in the spring or early summer. People did tend to avoid planning big events during hurricane season, which ran from June to November. But weddings near the coast were almost a year-round thing in the *Englisch* world. Sara had always wanted a spring wedding, so she'd picked the last Saturday of May, just *before* hurricane season.

"We're hungry," Carol said. "We played a ton of games and shuffleboard at the park, but we heard thunder so we came home."

"And invited others, I see," Lilah said, already grabbing the bread and peanut butter. "I'll make lemonade."

She glanced outside and saw a dark cloud forming over the trees. A normal afternoon pop-up shower. It was nice to see Carol and Dana with their girlfriends and a few boys at that. They'd already started going to youth frolics. Soon they'd be grown and married. Where would that leave her?

Her gaze moved on its own out to the man working on the gazebo. She'd be a lonely old widow—that's what would happen to her.

Sara groaned and shouted at Dana, "Stop running." She went to her room and shut the door. She'd need to change that attitude once she had her own *kinder*. Lilah wondered how Abram felt about having *kinder* right away. The man was methodical and he was marrying an impulsive, spur-of-the-moment girl.

Bless them, Lord, she prayed.

The group of teens giggled and headed to the back of the house, while Lilah made sandwiches, found a bag of chips, then sliced small chunks of pound cake. She glanced up and saw Noah hard at work and her smile widened, her heart lifting like a bird in flight. This gazebo might be a *gut* thing after all. Lilah hummed a tune and kept smiling. Until she turned and saw Sara had returned to the kitchen, her expression full of hurt and confusion. What was going on with this child?

Chapter Three

Noah finished up a few minutes before the rain hit. He'd marked off the spot in the yard where the gazebo would go and cleared the ground with a shovel and some fancy foot-patting. Now the circle of fresh earth would soon have a round foundation for the structure. It would be octagon-shaped and dainty, a white and bright Victorian style with three-foot-high railings all around the opening and steps leading up to benches inside. Lilah would have plenty of spots below the high-beamed dome ceiling to hang flowers or grow vines.

He'd make an ornamental top—a small replica of the gazebo's top. Then he'd crown it with a fancy finial. He'd find something intricate and meaningful to place on top of his creation. He had some nice curlicue corner brackets in his warehouse that he'd use to decorate the sturdy poles that would hold the whole thing up. It should have that wedding cake, Victorian theme that women seemed to love.

Having figured out that much, he'd bring his supplies tomorrow and get started on laying the blocks to set up the foundation. He should get the poles installed tomorrow, too. If he worked several hours a day, he'd be able to finish this in plenty of time for the wedding.

And beyond.

But today the rain had brought his work to a halt. Even though he'd finished most of the grunt work, which required digging and rearranging dirt to make a level place for the structure, he would have liked to clear the space a little more. He also wanted to make a flower bed around the gazebo for small plants. Colorful perennials or maybe pretty annuals to complement the camellia and azalea bushes surrounding the white picket fence of the backyard.

Whatever Lilah decided. Women loved flowers. He knew that from watching Janeen in their garden. She loved to grow flowers and produce, so much so that they had to can and freeze more food than they'd ever be able to eat. He didn't grow vegetables anymore. Most of the time, he either ate supper at one of the local restaurants, or he came home and had soup and a grilled cheese sandwich. Too many memories everywhere he glanced.

He was making a new memory today, however. One that involved another woman. He'd done work all over this part of the Florida peninsula, but he'd never taken to anyone in the way he'd taken to Lilah Mehl. Which had him on edge. So he gathered his tools and headed for his golf cart buggy, hoping to beat the worst of the rain home.

His work phone buzzed just as he rounded the corner of the house. "*Ja*, Gregory," Noah said, after seeing the familiar number. His foreman. "What's going on?"

"Boss, we got a problem with unit sixty-five at the Cedar Beach development," Gregory Hudson said. The *Englisch* foreman was one of the best in the business and thorough on all accounts. He was also a *gut* man with a strong faith.

"What kind of trouble?" Noah asked while he tried to get out of the downpour of rain. He ran back to Lilah's big covered back porch, hoping no one would notice him there.

"The client says he wanted it bigger and that's what he paid for. I only see the two-bedroom floor plans and that's what we've been working on. At least we'd laid out the foundation, but we haven't cemented it yet. He showed up today and got madder than a wet hen at the crew. Said we'd messed up his home."

"Bert Randolph, I reckon," Noah replied, frustrated. "That man has given us trouble from the get-go. He wants things his way and he'd like us to slip cheaper materials in, but I've explained we're not just building homes, but strong Amish-built homes. He can't grasp that."

"I agree. But he pulled out his own set of plans and sure enough, he'd asked for a small third bedroom for his mother."

Noah shook his head, thinking this would delay construction and he'd have to eat the cost. "Okay—is there a way to add on a room without too much time and labor?"

"I think we can do that, but I'll have to see if we have a big enough lot. Could set us back and he wants it done sooner than later."

"We'll make it work," Noah said. "I'll meet you there first thing tomorrow. Meantime, I'll call Randolph and soothe him. If we have to build him a new house on a bigger lot, we'll figure that out. But I think we can make it work on the current lot. He already had a prime spot with a view of the bay and it's a bit larger than most."

"He did point that out," Gregory replied. "I'll do some measuring when this blow-through gets done. It's mud all over the place here."

"Same where I'm standing," Noah said, watching the mud forming in the nice neat circle he'd just created. "I'll call you after I talk to Bert Randolph."

He ended the call and turned to leave again, only to find Sara Mehl standing at the window staring at him. Noah waved. She kept glaring. What had he done to offend the bride-to-be?

After checking the teens gathered on the other side of the house, Lilah saw Sara staring out at the rain. Then she saw Noah standing on the back porch, the pouring rain splattering him with dampness.

"Sara, why haven't you invited Noah inside?" she asked, heading to the back porch to call out to him.

"I think he's about to leave," her daughter said, as still as a country mouse in the corner. "He can't work in the rain."

"Nonsense." Lilah went to the door and stepped out, the wind and mist chilling her. "Noah, *kumm*. *Kumm* inside."

Noah whirled and shook his head. "*Neh*, I'm soaked and I won't ruin your floors. This should blow over soon enough."

"I insist," she said, waving him toward the door. "I have clean towels, and I'll make you some *kaffe* or lemonade."

He still hesitated, but when a bolt of lightning flared to the east, he finally hurried toward her. "*Denke.*"

Lilah ushered him in, then turned to Sara. "Bring some towels from the washroom and pull out the cheese I bought at Detwiler's yesterday. Crackers are in the cabinet."

Her daughter did an eye roll as she hurried to the small room off the kitchen. When Sara came back, she practically threw the towels at Noah.

Lilah shot her a raised eyebrow glare, then turned back to him. "That's some downpour, ain't so?"

"It came on quick," he said, grinning. "Didn't mind a few drops when I was about to leave, but I got a work call and then the bottom fell out. I'd have been fine on the porch. I like watching the rain from the porch."

Lilah didn't say it, but so did she. "Well, for now, let's get you something warm to drink. Are you hungry? I don't recall seeing you have the noonday meal."

"I was still full of pound cake," he said. "I have crackers in my work buggy. Normally, I'm in my hauling truck, but since I live a few miles from here, I brought my cart today."

"Those carts come in handy," Lilah said, aware that Sara was staring darts at them. "You got a lot done today."

Noah sank down on one of the dining chairs

where Sara had placed yet another towel. "I got the ground ready. Tomorrow, weather providing, I'll lay the foundation. I can do a slab of concrete or just use poles cemented in and build the floor up off the ground a bit."

"I don't think I'd like concrete," Lilah admitted. "Although that might keep snakes and other critters from hiding underneath."

"If you'd like it raised a bit, I can build a skirt around the floor," he replied as Sara brought crackers, cheese and fruit to him, her head down, her frown barely hidden.

"I like that idea," Lilah said. "What do you think, Sara?"

Her daughter finally stopped fidgeting. "I think lattice would work for the skirt."

Noah shot Lilah a questioning glance, then turned back to Sara. "Are you sure? I can put a tight lattice facing around the bottom. Hard for anything to get in there except a few lizards and spiders. Or I can put brick there and cement it all together."

Sara glanced from him to her *mamm*. "I don't know," she said. "I mean, I wanted it for my wedding but it seems you and Mamm have already worked it all out."

"Sara?" A heated blush moved down Lilah's neck. "You will not be rude to the man you insisted I hire for this. Noah is your husband's boss. Do you want the gazebo or not?"

"I do," Sara said. "I also wanted to have a say in how it's built."

"That's my fault," Noah said, his brows lifted. "I consulted your mother and explained the plan to her because she owns the property here. Force of habit."

"But I could have been in on that," Sara replied. "So you two wouldn't be alone when discussing things."

"What does that matter?" Lilah asked, wondering if all brides became *deerich* at times. Sara was certainly acting foolish.

"I'm the bride," Sara said. "I'm an adult now. I have opinions and concerns."

"What exactly are you concerned about?" Noah asked, his tone soft and encouraging. "Are you afraid I'll make an ugly gazebo?"

"*Neh*," Sara said, her *kapp* trembling as she shook her head. "I'm afraid you'll make a beautiful structure and I won't be here anymore. I won't be able to enjoy it after all."

Realization hit Lilah like a wet palm frond. "You'll be married and in your own home. Are you having doubts, daughter?"

"A lot of doubts," Sara said, wiping her eyes. "But not about marrying Abram. More about how I'll miss the garden and this new gazebo and I won't be able to come to the window and see it every day." She touched her fingers to the strings of her *kapp*. "And I also can see that you'll be alone, Mamm. I know you've learned to live without Daed, but you and I are always doing things together. I'll miss that."

Giving Noah a knowing glance, Lilah said, "Sara, you're welcome here every day. Always. You know that. And you'll be right down the street in your new home. I understand this will be difficult, but you will always have me in your life. Like it or not. And you can stand by this window all you want. Always. Or better yet, have Abram build you a small gazebo or pavilion in your own garden. You can grow whatever you like there, too."

"But it won't be the same," Sara said, her gaze back on Noah. "You'll meet new people and you'll forget about me."

"Now you're being silly," Lilah said, standing to touch Sara's hand. "How could I ever forget my firstborn?"

"The same way you've forgotten Daed," Sara said. Then she burst into tears and ran to her room.

Noah stood, his food half-eaten. "The rain has died down. I can make it home."

Lilah nodded. "I'm not sure what's wrong with Sara, but I should go and talk to her. I'm sorry she's been so rude when she was the one who wanted you to do this."

"Don't be so hard on her," Noah said. "I think what she's trying to say is that she'll miss you and her sisters, and her home. The home you shared with her *daed*."

Lilah let that settle over her. Tears burned her eyes but she refused to shed them. "I can't see what's right in front of me. My daughter is worried about our family changing, about her life changing—for the better this time—but she's wishing her *daed* could be here to see her get married."

"I think so," Noah replied. "Maybe you could do something in his honor to reassure her. A token at the wedding or a gift to her that will keep him in her heart. And yours."

"I haven't forgotten him," Lilah said, a fist to her heart. "How could I ever forget the man I loved?"

Noah's eyes flared with an all-too-familiar grief. "I certainly understand, but I don't think Sara does. By having me build this gazebo, she's leaving you with a gift. But she also needs it as a distraction because she's mourning her father and her loss. Getting married is a *wunderbar gut* thing, but she wants this to be perfect and that could only happen if her *daed* was still alive. Me building this gazebo is no substitute for that. Just like you falling for another man could be no substitute for your husband."

"Of course not," Lilah said, shaking her head. "I'll go and talk to her. And I'll see you tomorrow."

"Only if you and Sara are sure of that. And you'd better clear it with her."

"I will. If things have changed, I'll get word to you."

She watched him as he went out the back door and rounded the corner. What had just happened here?

Did Sara resent Noah's presence here, or was Noah warning Lilah about something else, something that involved grief and a longing that could never be fulfilled?

Maybe this whole gazebo build was a bad idea after all.

Chapter Four

Lilah sent Carol and Dana's friends home and had the girls folding laundry and watching the lasagna she'd put in the oven earlier. Noah was gone and the rain had turned to a soft mist that glistened in the late afternoon light like sparkles on a quilt.

Now, she stood at Sara's bedroom door, taking in the stacks of gifts friends had delivered, and thinking this child, her wild child, had always been difficult. Dramatic and sensitive, tender and loving, but difficult. Abram had calmed Sara, and Lilah knew her daughter loved Abram. He'd be a great husband and father if Sara didn't run him ragged from the start.

Lilah let out a sigh and said a silent prayer for patience and wisdom. Something was off with Sara and she needed to find out before the wedding plans got any deeper. She knocked softly on Sara's door, determined to listen before she judged or interjected her opinions.

"*Kumm* in," her daughter said in a quiet voice that only brought Lilah more worries. Sara had always lived loud.

Lilah opened the door to the bright white room with the big windows overlooking the garden. Sara had one of the windows open, the screen damp with rain. She'd always loved the scent after a rain. When she was little, Sara loved to play in the rain. Lilah missed those days of happiness and innocence.

"How are you?" Lilah asked as she sank down on an old slipper chair she'd reupholstered in a soft mint color.

Sara turned from her wedding notebook and stared over at Lilah. "I'm sorry, Mamm. I guess I'm tired."

"From work or from the wedding plans?"

Her daughter shut her journal and slipped it into the desk drawer. "Both."

"Are you happy, Sara?"

Sara's shocked expression was so earnest, Lilah knew it to be sincere. "I'm happy, of course. But I've never liked change. It's been hard lately with so much going on." She shrugged. "I guess I want it all to be perfect and that's a big want."

Lilah reached over to where Sara sat by her study desk. "That is the truth. Perfection is hard to come by and trying to make it so can ruin a lot of plans." She took Sara's hand. "I'll miss you, but you know I'll always be right here. On that account, nothing will change and nothing has to be perfect."

"You can't promise that, Mamm," Sara replied, her eyes bright with a deep hurt. "Things do change. Daed isn't here. You know I've dreamed of this wedding, and now, I don't have my *daed* here to witness it and be part of it."

"He knows, *liebling*. He will be here." Lilah touched her hand to Sara's heart.

Sara wiped her eyes. "I believe that, but I became afraid after begging for a gazebo. Would Daed resent that? Would he have built a gazebo if I asked for one on a whim?"

"Your *daed* would have given you the world," Lilah said. "He only wanted the best for his girls—that you all follow our faith and our beliefs and that you find happiness in your marriages."

"But how would he feel about another man, a stranger, building something in his yard?"

Lilah sat still after her daughter's question. She didn't know how to answer that. So she asked a question instead. "Do you regret asking for the gazebo, or is it that you've gone into a panic because someone else is building it for us?"

Sara stood and stared over at Lilah. "I want the gazebo because of you, Mamm. I mean, as I said yesterday, it will be pretty during the wedding, but mostly, it will be yours forever after the wedding. But not built by your husband."

Lilah's heart beat a fast jig. "Ah, I see. Noah is a nice man, a good-looking man, about the same age as me, ain't so?"

Sara bobbed her head. "Exactly. I didn't think that part through and now I'm afraid I've put temptation right in front of your eyes."

"Sara!"

"You like him. I can see that," Sara said, her expression stern. "I was wrong to be so impulsive. We can stop this gazebo being built right now if you want. But do you want to keep Noah away, or do you like having him here?"

Lilah couldn't lie to her daughter, especially since she was the one being put on the spot like a child. "Me liking him or not has nothing to do with him building this structure in the yard. I'd be kind to anyone working here, no matter."

"No matter *what*?" Sara asked, stubbornly grinding each word out.

Lilah felt trapped, cornered by her daughter's fears and misguided concerns. "Sara, what are you implying?"

Sara's dark eyebrows went up and her expression stiffened. "I see the way you glance at each other."

Lilah didn't know how to deal with this, but

she aimed to stop it cold. "Listen to me, Sara. I'm being kind to the man you wanted me to hire to build something pretty in the backyard—for your wedding and for our enjoyment in the years to come. I only met Noah yesterday, but he's been nothing but kind and considerate of our feelings and how we want this structure to be put together. I've had two or three conversations with him. It's not like we're planning to run away together. You've got the wrong notion in your head. If I've been out of line in any way, I apologize and I will stay away from Noah while he's here."

"But the damage is done," Sara replied, her voice rising in a shrill panic. "He's noticed you and you for certain sure noticed him. He's a nice-looking man and you—you're so pretty, Mamm. I can understand how you two would hit it off, but I never dreamed I'd be instrumental in causing something like this."

"This something you are implying is a nothing, child," Lilah said. "So, stop interjecting what you think you know into what is really happening. Noah is a nice man, and *ja*, he's a handsome man. I did notice that. I've talked to him and we've both shared how we still grieve for our spouses. Neither of us is ready for anything beyond chatting on the back porch, do you understand?"

Sara sank back down onto her desk chair. "I hope that's true. I mean at your age and all. I don't think I'm ready for you and Noah to have anything other than a professional acquaintance."

A professional acquaintance?

Lilah bit back the words she wanted to speak. She'd be the one to decide about her personal life. She'd need to be the one who was ready for this kind of change in her life. And right now, she wasn't ready or willing for anything more than being kind to someone who was doing work for her family. Not in the middle of wedding plans and trying to keep up with her own meager earnings from selling plants and baking. Not now, maybe not ever. The very thought of a love life made her want to hide in her bedroom.

But then she thought about Noah and his calm, sure nature, and how he liked to sit on the porch when it was raining. He had blue eyes that shone like the deep ocean when he smiled and a nice head of hair with just a touch of gray sweeping through it.

Lilah reeled in her wayward thoughts.

Neh, not ever. It couldn't happen.

"Mamm, are you angry at me?"

She stood, frustrated and embarrassed after Sara had to bring her back from her thoughts. "Enough, Sara. You are taking out your wedding jitters on me. I'm trying to do the right thing here, but perhaps I caved to your wishes too quickly. I will let Noah know his services are not needed here after all."

Sara let out a gasp. "*Neh*, Mamm. Don't do that."

"Sara, stop being wishy-washy and tell me the truth. Are you afraid something might happen between Noah and me?"

Sara nodded. "I was, but I can see I was wrong. Leave him be about not finishing. I want him to do this for us. I will try to stay out of this from now on. I'm so sorry I doubted you."

"That's better," Lilah said. "I will not listen to this type of accusation again, do you understand?"

"*Ja*, Mamm, I do," Sara replied, her head down. "You're right. I have the jitters. Weddings are complicated."

Lilah softened her tone. "They do tend to bring out the best and the worst—all the stress and all the emotions. But we are keeping this simple because we are very near the last bit of our budget. You will have a pretty wedding, gazebo or no gazebo. Some would frown on that anyway, but it's a nice gesture. I'm looking forward to enjoying it when I'm lonely."

Sara's neutral face turned to one of fear and panic again. "So you admit you're lonely then?"

Lilah shook her head and turned to leave. "I have admitted nothing. You're the one who seems to think I'm so lonely I'd latch on to the first man who's been in this house in years. Stop that and focus on your marriage and what's to come next. How about that?"

Lilah left Sara standing there, but she heard Sara's gasp. Her daughter had a lot to learn about love and marriage. If only her Joshua could be here to control these girls. She'd tried with all her might to keep them on the straight and narrow, to teach them right from wrong and to make sure they had food and shelter, faith and love. And whatever else it took to make a girl into a woman.

Sara's accusations hurt, but Lilah couldn't deny she'd felt something different after meeting Noah. And that something different scared her. It had come like a spark of fire and if she didn't keep it under control, she'd be the one in trouble. She couldn't let that fire burn. Her daughters would always come first and if Sara had already picked up on something stewing between Lilah and Noah, things could only go downhill from here.

Two days later, Noah whistled while he helped Tanner Dawson load wood onto the back of Noah's old pickup truck. Tanner had called him to let him know he had some leftover pine from a previous project, and he'd sell it to Noah with a big discount just to get it out of his storage building.

"You're in a *gut* mood today," Tanner said, grinning at Noah. "Something up with you?"

Noah heaved a breath and wagged a finger at the younger man. He considered Tanner a friend and like a son. Tanner and his wife Eva had helped Noah through the worst time of his life—when Janeen had passed. But he couldn't tell Tanner why he felt so alive today.

Because that had to do with another woman and Noah was having a hard time dealing with his feelings toward that woman.

"I'm enjoying this job, is all," he replied, telling that much of the truth. "I haven't built a fancy gazebo in years. Janeen always wanted one in our yard, but you know the saying about the cobbler having no shoes?"

Tanner's eyes filled with understanding. "You were too busy with work to build it?"

"*Ja*, and the irony of that is now I take on these side builds to keep my grief away. I should have made her one."

Tanner wiped his hands on his work pants and stared across at Noah. He'd gone through his own grief when his first wife had died too young. "Lilah Mehl is a nice woman. Eva used to help babysit her daughters when they were younger. Now Lilah's firstborn is getting married. Time flies."

"It does," Noah said. "And it's flying right now while we talk." He went back to loading wood and hoped Tanner would let it go at that.

"Well, do you like Lilah? Is that why you're whistling?"

Noah should learn not to whistle outside his home. "I like building her a nice structure in her lovely garden. It's springtime and her yard is blooming in all kinds of colors. And she fed me the biggest slice of almond-flavored pound cake."

"I've had Lilah's pound cake," Tanner said. "It's amazing. So you do like her?"

"I like her, *ja*," Noah admitted. "But mostly, I like that cake."

They laughed, but Tanner nodded and smiled at him. "It's nice to see you being so carefree, *mei* friend."

Noah smiled back and then he laughed. "I guess I have been morose and grumpy for a long time."

"You've been grieving," Tanner said. "A big difference. All the same, I'm glad you're enjoying your work, for whatever reason."

Tanner shot Noah another meaningful grin

before he turned to go back to work in his driftwood shop behind Dawson's Department Store.

Noah waved as he cranked the truck and headed a few blocks east to Lilah's house. And he started whistling again.

He did like Lilah, but he knew he'd have to be careful to keep things light between them. He hadn't thought of another woman since Janeen's death, and he never dreamed of remarrying, either. But he could enjoy Lilah's company and any food she offered him. Baching wasn't the most fun thing in the world.

Besides, they got along great and if Sara would quit being so moody and erratic and let him get on with his work, things could only get better from here.

Chapter Five

Something was wrong.

Noah knew it the moment he entered the front yard driveway of Lilah's home. The house stood on a street not far from Philippi Creek, so he could see shimmering water and heavy tropical foliage from the front porch. He liked the lay-out of the front yard. Not too big, with tower-ing palms on each side of the smaller porch here and rows of colorful annuals and perennials in neat beds across the lattice skirting underneath the porch. Rocking chairs and blossoms made the whole place welcoming.

The something wrong was that Lilah had not come out to greet him. Of course, he'd missed two days of showing up because of trying to calm down both his developer and the client who wanted to add another bedroom to his Lantz Seaside Cottage. Bert Randolph was a bitter man with money to burn. Noah had re-worked the original design to meet Randolph's standards and to correct the mistake someone on his construction team had made.

Randolph now would have one of the nicest seaside cottages Noah had ever created and still wanted to know if they'd throw in a complete landscaping at no charge. The yards weren't that big or that hard to maintain. Noah was still pondering on whether to give in or tell Bert Randolph he'd done all he could do to make amends.

He'd need to make amends with Lilah, too, he reckoned. He'd work double-time to catch up, and he should have factored that in when he'd agreed to do this.

Was she upset that he'd missed precious time on this project after only being here one full day? He should have sent word to her, but he'd gotten busy and hadn't thought about it.

Maybe she'd gone off on her cart to run errands this morning or walked to a nearby store as most here did on a nice early-summer day. Not that he expected her to rush out and greet him, but that first day she'd seen him through the window and then she'd suggested pound cake and *kaffe*. Just being kind and getting to know him, probably.

Noah decided he'd get to work and stop worrying because that wasn't getting the job done. A reminder that he usually didn't get involved in his clients' lives.

The house stood still and silent, so he went around to the side to open the white wrought-iron gate, since she'd given him permission to come and go as needed.

Then he saw her in the garden, bent over a lovely salmon-colored rosebush bursting with lush blooms. Noah couldn't deny it—the woman was pretty. She had golden-brown hair with a touch of gray moving through it like a rogue wave, and her eyes were a deep green that rivaled the palm fronds waving all around them. She wore a fuchsia-colored dress with a bright white apron and surprisingly, her tennis shoes had sunflowers sprinkled all over them.

"Lilah," he called, so as not to scare her.

She looked up and that's when he saw the something wrong. She frowned at him, and he instantly missed her pretty, welcoming smile. So she was aggravated with him already. Not a good start to his day.

Wiping her hands and putting her clippers in a small straw basket she'd placed on a small wooden bench, she said, "Noah. I wasn't expecting you today."

He nodded, acutely aware she seemed uncomfortable. "I'm so sorry I didn't get back until now. I had a situation with a client—always something when we're developing new neighbors. I should have sent word."

"That's fine." She glanced at the circle of fresh earth he'd left during the rain. "It's a nice day. You can get busy now."

She turned to leave but he called after her. "I'm truly sorry. I'll work double-time to get this done."

"It's not that," Lilah said, turning back to face him. "I have a busy day and well, I won't have time to chat much, and I know you'll understand and work hard yourself. I'll put a thermos of lemonade and some cookies on the porch for you."

Noah knew a brush-off when he saw one. "I think I do understand. I'll try to stay out of your way."

She gave him a glance that indicated she wanted to say more. "*Ach*, *vell*, I'll let you get to it then."

"*Denke*," he replied, wishing he knew what he'd done to make her so standoffish. Better not to ask, he decided. He'd learned one thing from asking a woman personal questions.

He might not like the answers.

He needed to stay away from her, too. His head was still spinning from first being around the woman. It occurred to him that maybe she was having some of the same unsettling feelings.

Lilah might want to avoid him for the very

reasons he felt he should avoid her. Grief. That could work both ways considering how much they both had going on in their lives. No time for small talk or any talk really. Like him, she probably was still in her own deep grief even though her husband had been dead a decade or so, from what he'd heard. This wedding would have stirred up all those old wounds and hurts.

That could be what was bothering Sara the most, too, as he'd suspected. Better to stay out of this situation.

Noah decided he'd go about his business and try his best not to think of Lilah. He had enough on his mind to keep him busy all day. He went back out front and pulled his truck close to the open gate, then started moving his supplies to the area he'd already sectioned off. Today, he'd dig holes and pour cement to mount the supporting poles. He'd cover the buried cement with dirt so it would never be seen. While the cement set, he'd start with the floor, spreading the narrow pine slats in a round pattern that would look like a starburst.

He started his work and soon was deeply involved in measuring and packing the wet cement that would support the poles for years to come. It was fast-drying and the heat and sun made it set very quickly, so he kept on with other tasks.

But when he heard the back door open and then shut, he glanced up and saw the promised lemonade and a plate of cookies on the bistro table. Maybe it was time for him to take a break.

But he'd try real hard not to think about the woman who didn't want to be around him. The way she'd shoved that food out the door, Noah reckoned Lilah had decided she wanted this work over and done.

And she wanted him out of her hair for good.

That shouldn't sting, but it did. He went to the porch and carried her offerings out to a nice old live oak. The oak provided shade while he took a break and tried not to think about the woman inside the house.

Lilah went about her cleaning with every breath she took, scrubbing, scouring, washing and dusting. Anything to keep her thoughts off the man sitting outside under her favorite oak tree.

She needed a bench under that tree. Then two people could sit there together. Not her and Noah, of course. But the girls and their friends. It would be nice for Sara and Abram to sit there after they'd married. Lilah could use the bench, too. It would be a great place to relax and stare at the gazebo once Noah was finished. Or now if she had nothing else to do but sit and watch someone else work. She could sneak out there after he left each day, of course. That would work.

"Only I can't afford a bench," she murmured while she dusted a side table in the sparse living room—a room she'd pieced together with flea market finds and scraps of bargain materials. She thought of Joshua and wished for the thousandth time he hadn't died so young. He'd helped her refurbish chairs and make curtains from nothing-much fabrics. He'd walked with her up and down flea markets and yard sales, and mud sales when they visited family up North.

"We have a little money," he'd always say. "Let me buy you something nice."

"I can make things nice without spending too much money," she'd reply.

"And for that I am forever grateful."

Then they'd laugh and get ice cream.

He knew she'd come from a poor family and that she believed in making every dollar go a long way. He always told her that being frugal was one of her sweetest traits, because she didn't use it as a weapon, but as a tool.

"I need you here," she whispered as she remembered him trying to make her a bench when they were first married. It came out crooked and some of the grooves didn't line up, but how she'd loved that bench. It finally fell apart a few years after he'd passed and when she'd spotted it, all broken apart, she'd sat down on the grass next to it and had herself a *gut* cry. She might cry now, because her life had become broken, the same as that old bench.

Or she could gather her thoughts and go out and see if Noah needed anything. Would Sara disapprove of her checking on him?

She couldn't blame this hesitation completely on Sara. Lilah felt such a deep guilt, as if she were being unfaithful to Joshua. She knew that was silly since a lot of Amish widows found new husbands. Many women could find someone new without remorse, so why was she so worried about just talking to another man? It wasn't as if she had plans to marry again. She'd made that decision the day Joshua died. He'd left her with a little money from selling the family farm back in Lancaster County, but she still had to find ways to make ends meet. His bad heart and then joint problems had brought him South to the warmer weather, and of course, she'd come with him. Sara had just turned four-years-old when they'd moved, and four years later, Carol came along, followed by Dana three years later. Shortly after Sara's tenth birthday they'd found out his heart condition was too far gone for any further treatment. He died three months later.

Explaining his illness and death to her young daughters had been the hardest thing she'd ever done. Joshua had a great job working for one of the local produce markets. He helped gather the vegetables and fruits and brought them fresh to the markets every day. He loved being a Florida farmer. And when he passed, many of his *Englisch* co-workers had come to show their respect. He was that kind of man.

Finished with the housecleaning, unless she started all over again, Lilah sank down on a stool in the kitchen and held her head in her hands. She said a silent prayer, thanking *Gott* for allowing her to have a few precious years with her husband. Then she asked the Lord to help her get through this wedding and raise her younger daughters so they could be married and happy, too.

And let me avoid any temptations, Lord, please, she prayed.

When she glanced up, she saw Noah standing at the back door, staring at her.

Lilah stood so quickly, the table next to her wobbled. Her heart fluttered from surprise and a new feeling she didn't want to recognize. Hurrying to the door, she opened it and said on a breath of air, "Was there something you needed?"

Noah gave her a questioning stare that said so many things, she wasn't sure what would happen next. Then he cleared his throat and held up an empty glass and plate. "Just this—*denke*. That hit the spot."

"*Ja*, of course." She took the plate and glass but didn't invite him in.

He tugged at his straw hat and straightened it. "Ah, Lilah, would you like to see the progress on the gazebo? I know you want to be left alone, but I need to make sure you like it so far. Do you have a minute?"

She had all the time in the world but she couldn't say that. She checked the stove where she had already turned down the burners on supper tonight. Fresh vegetables cooked with tiny bits of ham, biscuits she'd baked this morning. She had no excuses.

"I do have a few minutes before Carol and Dana return from a frolic down the street. And Sara will be home later. She was meeting with Abram to talk about what else needs to be done on their house."

He nodded and gave her another glance. "So we won't be interrupted?"

"*Neh*, but even if we were, it would be okay. I mean, it's not like I can't *kumm* out and see what you're up to, ain't so?"

"I hope you can do that, *ja*. It's a nice day

and it's still broad daylight. Best time to see the project before the sun goes down."

She sat the dishes on the counter and turned to follow him, wishing she hadn't been so rude earlier, but she whirled too fast out the door and almost ran into him. Their eyes met and that funny feeling hit her again, causing her to feel light-headed and giddy.

Noah caught her and steadied her, his arms strong and sure, his hands still warm from the sun. "Are you all right?"

"Just dizzy—I mean—busy. I've cleaned the house all day. I have several friends coming tomorrow to finish up some details on the wedding meal."

"Are you feeling tired? Did you say dizzy?"

"*Neh.*" She managed a laugh. "Busy, just busy. I get my words mixed-up sometimes."

Apparently whenever a fine-looking man was holding her.

Noah stepped back and dropped his hands from her arms, his expression a map of worry and confusion. "Your home always smells like fresh lemons and mint, so don't overwork yourself."

"*Denke.*"

She beamed at his praise, then told herself to be more stoic. Her nerves jingled like a set of old keys, while her heart purred like a happy kitten. What was wrong with her?

Noah obviously thought something was wrong, too. "We can do this another time if you're tired or if you'd rather not," he said. But the disappointment in his words brought her out of her stupor.

She had to get control over these strange emotions. And now, before her daughters came home for supper.

"I'm fine," she replied. "Really, Noah, I've got so many things going on I am dizzy but in a *gut* way."

His answer sounded like a frustrated grunt, but he didn't say anything more about dizziness or busyness.

But surely he had to think she was *verhuddelt.*

Because she felt foolish, very foolish, right this minute. And she wasn't very good at trying to avoid him, maybe because she didn't want to avoid him. She'd need to pray on that matter.

Chapter Six

"Show me then," she said, hoping she sounded like the homeowner and not the woman who thought Noah Lantz was such a nice, good-looking available man that he'd made her dizzy.

He smiled and shook his head. "You are having wedding jitters, I reckon."

"I am," she replied, going with his assumption, relief in her heart and in her words. "It's just so hectic and of course my Sara comes up with new plans every day. I will do some serious praying for Abram. He will have his hands full with that one."

Noah laughed while they walked toward the back of the yard, the scents of jasmine and honeysuckle merging to perfume the air. "Is she feeling better today? She seemed on edge last time I was here."

"She has wedding jitters," Lilah said. "I'm surprised Abram hasn't mentioned her moods to you, but he protects her and loves her."

"He only talks about their marriage when I see him, which isn't often. He's a man in love."

Lilah wished she could explain this a bit more, but she held her tongue along with her thoughts and her awareness of Noah being here.

"She's fine. Always seeking perfection. I think because her *daed* died when she was young and impressionable. She's been trying to make up for that for years."

Noah turned to her after they reached the area where he'd been working. "And have you been doing the same?"

Confused, she asked, "What does that mean?"

"Have you been compensating because you are a single parent?"

Anger and shock coursed through her veins, but she held herself in check. "I've been trying to do the best I can with what *Gott* gave me. I'm not sure what else I can say."

Noah's eyes went soft with compassion. "I'm sorry. I've never had children, so I shouldn't be questioning how you're raising yours."

"*Neh*, you shouldn't," she said, accepting his apology. "I'm sorry you never had the opportunity to raise a child." Glancing back at the house, she added, "I was just thinking about Joshua. You know with the wedding coming, we all wish he could be here. I'm thankful for the years we had together but I miss him, especially at times like this."

Noah gave her a quizzical stare, his face pinched with his own pain. "I miss Janeen every day." Then he moved on, shaking off the cloak of grief. "I imagine it's not easy raising three children alone," he said, clearly uncomfortable now. "Let's get back to the work at hand, something I do know about."

She nodded, but the cheery moments were gone. Noah hadn't been around her and her girls enough to make judgments about how she had raised them. His questioning words stung like cold water being thrown in her face. But he was right; he'd never been a *daed*, so he didn't know all the many emotions a parent had to deal with on a daily basis. He would make a *gut daed*, she imagined, her thoughts going off on a walk of their own.

But she did a hard stop on that and got herself back on track. She'd continue to avoid him unless he needed her to check on things while he worked. She wouldn't let someone she barely knew tell her how to raise her daughters or question how she'd gone about it. Hadn't she paid the price of being alone? Hadn't she tried to do right by her family?

Noah gave her a moment and then explained how he'd set up the poles by surrounding them with cement that would harden and keep them steady. "It's already good and dry, and solid. Only a hurricane could knock them over, but it would need to be a strong one at that."

"I've heard rumbling that one or two are already forming way out the Gulf. I hope the wedding is over before any big storms approach the Florida peninsula."

"We can only hope," he replied, glancing at the sky. "Pop-up showers later today, probably."

Lilah nodded and then studied the eight thick wooden posts that stood straight and steady in an octagon-shaped circle toward the open sky. "I love the round posts. So you'll build the rest around this foundation?"

"That's the plan," Noah said. "I'll paint it white using a heavy-duty weatherproof paint and I'll add intricate lacy filigree cornices against the top of the posts. What do you think?"

"I'm not sure," she admitted. "I don't know much about construction. As long as it's built on solid ground."

"It is," he said. "I can assure you of that." Then he let out a grunt of a sigh. "I've offended you and I'm sorry."

Lilah blinked back tears of fatigue and grief. She refused to have a meltdown. She wasn't a meltdown-type person.

Embarrassed, she took a breath and lifted her chin. "It's all right, Noah. I'm sure I've made mistakes with my girls and you probably see that, being an outsider, and especially with Sara getting her way so much."

"I'm not one to judge," he replied. "I just wonder what it's like to have to watch over those three and do it right. I admire you for that and I imagine you are weary at times. But as you know, Janeen and I never had *kinder*. It's a regret for certain sure, but I never let her know my regrets."

Lilah's heart softened again. She didn't need to be rude to him because he'd made an observation regarding her daughters. Why was she so emotional and all over the place these days?

"It's not easy," she said, her tone soft and full of defeat. Then she shook her head. "It's hard at times, but we do what we must. You're seeing Sara at her worst. She's always been anxious and she doesn't handle change very well. Marriage is a big change. I'm trying to guide her without upsetting her."

"But she's upsetting you, ain't so?"

"I'm a mother, Noah. Worry comes with the territory."

"That is true—from what I've seen and heard." He gave her a look that indicated he understood. "Let's change the subject to one I know. I hope you like the work so far. I've lingered too long."

Now he looked offended. She wished she didn't show her emotions so much. "I appreciate your work," she said, but her words sounded lame. She placed a hand on his arm. "You've done a great job so far, Noah. It's just that—"

Noah's eyes went dark as he stepped toward her. "What is wrong?"

Then the back door burst open and Sara came running out into the yard. "Mamm, there you are. Carol fell playing dodgeball and we think she might have sprained her ankle."

Lilah gasped and turned to Noah. "I have to go."

He nodded and whirled with her. "I'll help. I can drive you to the ER."

"*Neh*, you'd better just go on home, Noah. I can handle this. I have a cart or I'll call a taxi."

Lilah rushed toward the house, all the while aware of her daughter's disapproving stares along with Noah's disappointed glances.

She couldn't please either of them right now.

Two hours later, Lilah sat with Carol on the couch, an ice pack in her hand. "Keep that on your foot," she told her daughter, "and keep your foot elevated. It's not a bad sprain but you don't need to be walking on it just yet."

"I have plans," Carol wailed, shaking her head as she touched the tight gauze the nurse had wrapped around her ankle. "Summer is here now and you promised we could go the beach with the youth group. You know, our Mennonite friends invited us. I can't miss that." Carol's brown eyes watered. "I might miss the wedding if I can't walk."

"You can't walk or swim," Sara said as she placed supper on the table. "You'll be fine by the time the wedding gets here. I heated this food up so let's eat."

"Sara, I don't like your tone," Lilah replied. Her eldest had been giving her the silent treatment since she'd returned from the ER with Carol. Dana had stayed to help Sara warm up supper. Now her youngest glanced from mother to daughter, a worried frown creasing her forehead.

"What is going on?" Dana finally said. "Sara, who are you mad at today? Mamm or Abram? It's always one or the other and sometimes both."

Sara dropped the bright yellow potholder she'd used and stared at Dana. "Right now it's you. That was not a nice thing to say."

"Well, you're not acting nice at all," Dana replied. "Carol is hurt and Mamm is tired. Can't you see anything beyond your nose?"

Sara glared at her little sister. "*Ja*, I can see a lot happening around here and none of it is *gut*."

Lilah stood and held her knuckles tight against the table. "All right, that is enough. We've had a busy, trying day and Carol is tired. Stop this bickering and let's eat our supper."

"It's been reheated," Sara replied, her gaze zoomed in on Lilah like radar. "Mamm left it to go out and admire the gazebo."

And there it was again. That resentment, that passive anger her daughter had been carrying around for the last few days. Lilah wondered how to handle this.

"We will eat," she said. "Carol, I'll bring you a plate to the couch, so don't get up."

Carol nodded, fatigue darkening her eyes. "*Denke*, Mamm."

Sara grunted and poured their iced tea, her bottom lip jutting out all the while.

After Lilah filled a plate of turnips, tomatoes and creamed corn with a buttery biscuit for Carol, she and Dana sat down. Sara finally joined them, her expression stern. They all bowed their heads and said their silent prayers. Lilah asked *Gott* to show her how to handle her confusing daughter. She wished she knew why Noah's presence seemed to upset Sara so badly. Her daughter's protests against her speaking to another man besides Joshua had shaken her to the bone and made her even more stubborn in having innocent conversations with him while he worked. Noah had to think they'd all lost a few marbles with the way they'd treated him.

Was there something wrong with her having a male friend, a man who was kind and considerate and respectful even if he didn't have a clue about raising children?

Sara stared at her food, then finally glanced up at Lilah. "I'm sorry, Mamm, but I don't like you being around Noah so much."

"That, my daughter, is obvious," Lilah replied. Then she glanced from Sara to Dana and then over to where Carol sat shocked on the couch.

"Sara, we discussed this earlier and you agreed that you would stop this nonsense. You implied you were just frazzled because of work and the wedding. Now, you act as if we never had that conversation."

She paused and took a breath, her heart beating too fast. She'd never been good at confrontations. But she needed to make them understand.

"I want all of you to know that I loved your father with all my heart and I miss him every day. But you also need to know that me visiting with Noah Lantz means nothing. He is working here because we invited him to do so." She shot Sara a stern glance. "You wanted this, Sara. You practically handpicked Noah."

Sara's chagrin changed to a stubborn frown. "To do work for us, Mamm. Not socialize."

"I think I can decide with who and when I can socialize, Sara," Lilah replied. "I had hoped you'd let this go and enjoy the next couple of weeks before you move out of this house."

"I'm trying to enjoy things," Sara said on a whimper. "I don't know what's wrong with me, but seeing you like this is disturbing."

Carol called from the sofa. "I don't feel disturbed, Mamm. It makes me smile."

Sara did an eye roll. "Everything makes you smile."

"She is a pleasant person," Dana chimed in. "Sara, you need to be happy about your future. Let Mamm take care of hers."

"What wise words," Lilah said, nodding toward Dana. "Dana is right. This gazebo will represent a happy time—Sara's wedding—and after that we will have many *gut* memories in the garden. We've all worked on this house and this yard and it's turned into a haven for me. Now, the gazebo will remind me of Sara's thoughtfulness and her wedding day, but it will also comfort me each time I look out the window. It's whimsical and unnecessary, *ja*, but now that it's being built, I'm really enjoying it and I can't wait to sit there inside the gazebo and have my mint tea or eat ice cream with all of you. I'm excited so I do go out and offer Noah food and drink, the same I'd do for anyone visiting our home. I'm happy because I have someone my age to talk to and listen to. He's a smart man and he is very kind, so I will not tolerate any of you being rude to him."

She glanced at Sara. "Do you all understand?"

"I like Noah," Carol said, needing to be a part of this conversation. She broke off a piece of flaky biscuit and dipped it in her turnip juice. "He's handsome and being in your mid-forties doesn't mean you can't look at a man, Mamm."

"*Denke*, Carol," Lilah said. "You and your sister seem to grasp what I'm trying to say."

Sara lifted her head and glared at Carol. "Who gave you that impression? Mamm is a widow. She doesn't—she shouldn't be—ready to look at another man. We need to focus on my wedding and this is a distraction."

Dana snorted. "Are you serious, Sara? You're getting married and you don't want the same for Mamm?"

"She's too old to be flirting," Sara replied, her tone so judgmental it was almost comical.

"She's a pretty woman," Carol said, wincing when she moved her foot too quickly. "And she's not too old. Widows do remarry, you know."

"I know that," Sara said, getting up to throw

her food in the trash. "And that's what scares me the most."

Lilah sat shocked and still. She didn't like being reprimanded by her daughter, but Sara was Sara. She was opinionated and outspoken and a bit spoiled.

Could it be Noah was right, after all? Had she been overcompensating because of Joshua's death?

Sara turned to stare at her. "Do you like him, Mamm?"

"I do," Lilah admitted. "I truly do. But that doesn't mean I'm ready to run away with him."

Carol started giggling. "That would be funny, seeing you and Noah running down the street, Sara chasing you with her fist in the air."

"Not so funny," Sara replied, but she had a twitch going on with her lips. "I'd get the cart to chase them."

Dana held her hand over her mouth, she was laughing so hard. "You'd run that cart into a palm."

Lilah grinned, then took Sara's hand. "Will you trust me, please? I am a grown woman after all and I am still young by most standards. I can make my own decisions regarding love."

Sara's smile died a little but then she perked back up. "I'm getting married in three weeks. I'll try to have a *gut* attitude about everything."

Then she shrugged. "I just wasn't expecting you and Noah to become such *gut* friends. I know I flounder about this, and I think I can handle it until I see you two together. I've never seen you flirt, Mamm."

Lilah didn't know how to respond to that.

"Try to see that as a *gut* thing," Carol called out. "I have a sprained ankle, but I'm perfectly fine with Mamm flirting with Noah. What can it hurt?"

Sara glanced at Lilah again. "I don't know, and I hope no one will get hurt. That's all."

Lilah hadn't thought about getting hurt. How could forming a friendship with a male friend hurt her?

Or was Sara afraid she'd be the one who'd wind up hurt?

"Let's end this discussion," she said. "Sara, try to contain your disappointment. You and I will talk again later."

Carol sent Dana a speaking look, meaning they'd talk about this later, too. Alone, together. They were hearing too much adult conversation. She'd have to spend more time with her two younger girls.

And apparently, less time flirting with Noah Lantz.

Chapter Seven

The next day, three of Lilah's friends arrived to finish up the wedding details. Amish traditions sometimes involved the new couple living with their parents until their home was ready. Abram and Sara would stay with his parents for a week or so since their house was still being renovated. Thankfully, Samuel and Betty Troyer had a roomy home on a quiet street near the park. Sara got along great with her future in-laws. Another blessing. But Lilah would miss her so much, moods and all. Maybe once Sara was married and putting together her own home, she'd settle down and give Lilah some breathing room.

Meantime, Lilah's friends were helping with all the household needs a young bride might want—quilts and linens, curtains and washable napkins and dish towels, dishes and pots and pans.

"I have the food under control," Ramona

Bauer said. "I know you'll be too busy to cook a meal, Lilah, so don't worry about things. Eva and Martha will both help me in the kitchen here."

"You are too kind," Lilah replied. "I will help where I can, of course."

Ramona ran a tea shop that had become quite popular with both Amish and *Englisch* women. She'd offered to put the traditional meal together and she'd given Lilah a discount on the food—as a gift to the happy couple and mostly as a gift to their longtime friendship.

"You can focus on the gathering in your yard," Ruth Kohr said. "Adina and Eva will help with whatever you need." The two younger women were now married and living happily with their husbands in Pinecraft.

Ruth ran a quilting and sewing shop a few blocks east of Lilah's street. Adina was Ruth's new daughter-in-law. Her son Nathan had married Adina last year after he'd helped Adina find her missing sister, Blythe. Blythe had gone back to Campton Creek for a few months. Adina and Nathan lived with Ruth over the quilting shop in a lovely apartment.

"Where is Sara?" Ruth asked, glancing around. "I expected her to be here to see our handiwork."

"She should arrive any moment," Lilah

said. "She's still working at that new café. The Beachside Café. The place is so cute and has a beach theme, but her boss is moody and demanding."

She didn't mention Sara had been the same lately.

"I hear the owner is a tyrant," Ramona said. "I've had return customers who say they'll never go back there because he's so rude."

"I hear stories each time she comes home." Lilah let out a sigh. "She's been edgy and fretful for a week now."

"Weddings," Martha, a cousin to Tanner Dawson, said. "The brides are always fitful at times."

Lilah nodded. "Our bride has been skittish and all over the place with her whims and mood. Sara decided she wanted a gazebo built in the backyard, so that's happening as we sit here."

"*Ach*, *vell*," Ramona said. "Isn't that a fine idea."

"She says it's for me, after she's gone," Lilah explained. "But she thinks it will be a nice backdrop for her wedding. Is that too much, do you think? Frivolous and prideful, ain't so?"

"It's a nice gesture," Ruth said. "I think your yard is so pretty and that would be a beautiful addition." She stood and stretched after they'd finished folding pretty yellow sunflower-embossed napkins and boxed up the plain white dishes for Sara and Abram. "Who's the builder out there?"

Lilah got up out of her chair too quickly and almost knocked over a tray of small sandwiches they'd had for the noon meal. She'd forgotten all about Noah coming today.

"He looks familiar," Martha said. "Hey, I know him. He's *gut* friends with Tanner. That's Noah Lantz. Tanner told me Abram is working for him now."

An embarrassed heat rushed over Lilah as her friends scurried like curious cats to the kitchen window and then turned back to her. "*Ja*, and I just found that out when Sara invited him to come and measure before she discussed the gazebo with me. I need to pay more attention to my daughter's chatter. She mentioned the new job, but apparently forgot to mention the man who gave Abram the job."

"He's a looker," Ramona said, chuckling. "And he's got money. He builds the cutest little homes all along here. Lantz Seaside Cottages, as the signs say."

They all stayed there staring at Lilah, their expressions begging her to tell all.

She cleared her dry throat and wished she could melt into the floor. "I…uh…know about his work, but Sara said Abram suggested him, and she somehow convinced me to hire him. He told me he likes to do these side jobs because he enjoys creating pretty structures. He does them alone. It helps him with his grief. His wife died of cancer three years ago."

"I'd heard that," Ruth replied, studying Lilah. "You and he are about the same age, ain't so?"

"What does that matter?" Ramona asked, glancing from Noah to Lilah. Then she said, "Oh, I see." Her smile widened. Ramona loved a good scoop on anything romantic.

"See what?" Lilah ran to the window. Noah lifted a beam over his shoulder as if it were a sack of potatoes. He was muscular and solid, that was for certain sure. "What do you see, Ramona?"

"I see a match," Ramona replied. "A perfect match. I'm guessing we might have another wedding here in the future. A wedding with a gazebo in it."

Lilah put a hand to her blushing face, then dropped it. "You can't talk like that around Sara. She does not like me being kind to Noah. She accuses me of flirting with him."

"Well, what woman wouldn't?" Martha edged forward. "You know, there are a lot of lonely widows around here, some in this very room."

They all looked at Lilah. She shook her head.

"Would you stop? I'm serious about Sara. She's not happy, but she's the one who asked him to build that gazebo. I'm wishing she'd left well enough alone."

Her three friends gave Lilah a speaking glance, their expressions holding questions she wasn't ready to answer.

Martha took her by the arm. "We shouldn't tease you. You loved Joshua, we know. It's hard to change a heart set on that kind of love. It took Tanner a long time to get over his first wife and now he's so in love with Eva."

"Are you saying I should just forget Joshua then?" Lilah asked her friends, tears in her eyes.

"*Neh*," Ruth replied in a soft tone. "We're saying you have to be the one to decide what is best for you, keeping *Gott*'s will in perspective, of course."

"I don't think *Gott*'s will has anything to do with Noah building me a gazebo," Lilah replied. "Does it?"

Ramona touched her other arm. "That depends on which way your heart is leaning right now, Lilah." She smiled at Lilah, then turned to watch Noah. "Something prompted Sara to find the perfect person to build you a gazebo, and if she's having doubts now, well, that means she loves you and she's afraid of letting you go."

Lilah stood against the counter and stared

out at where Noah stood studying the foundation and flooring of the gazebo. "My heart is confused, hurting, wondering and wishing all at the same time. But I can't be that forward because I've only just met the man, and Sara's so against me even being friends with him. I've been avoiding him and I think I've hurt his feelings. He is so kind and considerate he is staying out of my way, but I have to admit I have enjoyed spending time with him."

"So your daughter is dictating your life now?" Martha asked with a frown.

"I'm trying to get through this wedding," Lilah replied. "I can't have another discussion with her about this. She's nervous and worried about me, but she's also happy and ready to have her own home and be with her new husband. I think if I ignore this situation, she'll settle down."

"Lilah is right," Ruth said, glancing at Noah as he hammered boards to make the floor of the gazebo. "The wedding is now two weeks away and Noah should be finished with this work by then. After that, who knows what might transpire. A supper invitation, a walk in the park, a nice cart ride to the bay?"

"Would you be more open then?" Ramona asked, true sympathy in her dark eyes, her round face full of hope.

"I might," Lilah admitted. "Right now, it's too much and too soon. I need to get to know him better. He's heartbroken, same as me, but we know our loved ones are with *Gott* now."

"And *Gott* knows the outcome of this before we even try to guess," Martha reminded them. "Still, we all could use a little romance to keep us on our toes. I'm happy for you, Lilah. You have your girls to consider."

"*Denke*," Lilah said. "I do consider them—all three of them. I'd never do a thing to hurt them or confuse them."

Ruth lowered her voice since Carol was upstairs resting her sprained ankle. "And how do Carol and Dana feel about Noah and you? Same as Sara?"

"They like him and seem okay with us being friends. I think they are fatigued with all the wedding planning, and so am I."

"It will be a joyful occasion, and then you will have some time to consider this new development in your life," Ruth said. "No need to rush things. You and Noah are past the age of puppy love. This can be a sweet companionship, if that's what you both want and if *Gott* guides your decisions."

Ruth had such a sincere face and a kind nature, Lilah felt better immediately. She trusted Ruth, Martha and Ramona. "You've all given me such *gut* advice," she said. "And Ruth, you went through so much last year, my problems seem like small potatoes."

"We had a very eventful summer last year, *ja*," Ruth replied, "but Nathan is happily married now and Adina is the best daughter-in-law I could ever ask for."

"Let's get back to Lilah and that interesting man who is headed this way," Martha said, inclining her head toward the backyard. "He might need some water or lemonade, Lilah."

"I can't take Noah any food or drinks," Lilah replied, her eyes on Noah. Tall, with that thick thatch of hair, he did make a striking figure. "Sara wouldn't like that at all."

"What wouldn't I like?" Sara asked from the front door, which Lilah had left open to get airflow. "Oh, let me guess." Her daughter hurried toward the big kitchen window. "You want to go and visit with him, am I correct?"

Lilah glanced at her friends and then she turned back to her daughter. "You are correct, Sara, but you will respect me while you're still in this house. Just like my friends here, Noah is a guest while he works here. I thought after we talked last night, we agreed you would control your feelings and we also agreed that Noah and I are friends. Now mind your manners and thank all these women for coming to help today.

Then we are all going out on the porch with lemonade and what's left of the wonderful tea sandwiches Ramona brought today."

Sara's face flushed red, but she didn't protest anymore. Instead, she gave Lilah an imploring glance. "May I have a couple of those sandwiches, too? I never got to take a break today."

Lilah sighed. "Of course you can have some food. Eat and then rest up. Oh, and take a plate up to Carol. After we feed Noah, we'll show you everything we got done today, okay?"

Sara smiled, but it looked as if someone had pinched her to make her do so. "*Ja*, and *denke* all for coming. I'm sorry I was grumpy from work, but I do appreciate your help so much."

The other ladies laughed and hugged Sara, and after she went out front to where the food was spread on the table, Martha grabbed Lilah by the arm. "*Gut* for you, friend. You stood up to what the *Englisch* would call a bridezilla. Now, let's go out and talk to that handsome Noah. We'll be your chaperones, ain't so?"

Lilah started chuckling, and soon they had a big plate of tiny crustless sandwiches and several tea cakes and cheese straws to take out to Noah.

When Lilah guided them all out onto the porch, he glanced up and looked puzzled, but made his way toward them in a slow steady gait.

"I'm not sure whether to be happy to see you all or run for my life."

That made all of the women chuckle and give each other sly glances. Lilah shot him a sympathetic silent apology, her skin feeling hot again. "We don't bite. We brought you some refreshments."

"Now that's more like it," Noah said, but he still didn't look so sure about this group.

Lilah had to admit the man was adorable when he looked afraid. But he had nothing to fear from her. Nothing at all.

Chapter Eight

Noah was still sitting on the porch steps after the ladies left. They'd made such a fuss over feeding him, and then after a bout of small talk about the weather and the gazebo, they'd made a great show of excusing themselves to go in and look over Sara's wedding fare. Noah had never been great at talking with women, but he knew the cues well enough to understand Lilah's friends were curious about him. Did they each think he was on the open market or something? Or were they asking him pointed questions on Lilah's behalf? Either way, he was exhausted and antsy and glad they had other things to distract them from watching him work the rest of the afternoon. He needed to make the rounds on the two developments going up not far from here, and he didn't want to be off his game with his crews.

The quiet he'd enjoyed while he finished eating ended when the door opened again. Lilah came out and sat down beside him, her smile endearing.

Ah, now this was much better.

She hesitated for a moment and then asked, "Did you like the food?"

He nodded, liking her delicate floral freshness even more. Did she wash her clothes in a batch of flowers?

He pointed to the empty plate on the table. "I have to admit, those were the tiniest chicken salad sandwiches I've ever seen. It took a half dozen of 'em for me to believe I'd even had a sandwich. And the grapes were a nice surprise."

She laughed and the melody of that lyrical sound made his heart hum right along with her. "They are rather dainty. Finger sandwiches is the correct term. Ramona's Tea Shop holds fancy tea parties for women. Her presentation is amazing and her cottage on the main avenue is so cute and welcoming. She explains everything about the tea and how to steep it and even how the food should be layered on the tiered trays she uses. It's amazing."

Noah decided just listening to Lilah talk was an amazing thing. He'd been so shut off from allowing himself to feel, to be happy again, that he'd forgotten how making small talk could be soothing. He talked to his employees all day, but rarely got to know any of them except the ones he'd known already. He'd change that tactic from now on.

"The sandwiches hit the spot and I still have all my fingers," he replied with a teasing grin while he held up his fingers as if counting them. "And the cheese straws were pretty tasty, too. But that giant white cookie was the best surprise."

Lilah tucked a strand of hair behind her ear, her *kapp* neat and clean. Her light blue dress looked like the sky over the ocean. "Oh, her white-chocolate almond cookies are the best. I could eat them for supper." She leaned close. "Sometimes, that's all I eat for supper. Cooking isn't my strong point."

Noah's breath left his body. He looked at her, his gaze holding hers. "*Your* food ain't bad, you know."

In fact, he wanted to tell her he could find nothing bad about her. But he had to stay the course and while being a friend, he also had to watch his step with Lilah.

As if she'd realized the same thing, Lilah stood up with a quick leap. "I'm not the best cook or housekeeper. Gardening is my favorite thing. Joshua used to tease me about that. But I can make a passable pot roast or chicken pot pie."

She stopped and glanced out over the yard in

a way that showed she wasn't ready for intimate conversations. "I wonder what he'd say about my garden now?"

Her words hit Noah with a deep yearning and a soft melancholy he recognized all too quickly. "I often wonder what Janeen would think of me now. My business started growing in an increasing rate the year before she died. I spent time working that I should have spent with her. She told me it was okay, but it wasn't. I should have gone with my heart and let work take care of itself."

Lilah's eyes held compassion and a startled pain. "She must have wanted you to stay busy, to do the work you love. And maybe she needed to let go a little bit, too, knowing how things would be in the end."

Noah stared over at the woman by his side and yearned to have a long talk about all of this. "Still, I should have spent every waking moment with her, and I did cut back. Those last few weeks, I stayed by her side and wished I'd done so sooner."

"I'm so sorry, Noah."

He stood, too, a wave of intense guilt making the food he'd eaten roil against his ribs. He wasn't really all that ready to talk, after all. "I should go."

Lilah didn't argue with him. "*Ja*, I'm sure you're exhausted."

They stood silent for a moment, the wind moving over them with a soft whisper, the sun gliding toward the night in a slow waltz, the sizzle of the warm day going cool while their gazes held a sweet heat.

Then she took a long breath. "Noah, I understand. We are both still lost in a world that went away the day they died. My memories have mellowed over the years, but yours are still fresh and new. It's like a knife never leaving your heart, a gash that will always be an open wound, a story that doesn't have an ending."

Noah swallowed the burning pain in his throat. "*Ja*, that's it exactly. That and the guilt."

They stayed a few feet apart, Lilah with her head down and her hands twisted against her apron, him with his hat in his hand and his heart shattering all over again. Noah didn't know how to comfort her because he had not learned how to comfort himself. But he prayed for peace and acceptance every day.

"So what do we do about all of that?" he finally asked, his voice husky with a river of emotions. "I mean—here we are, suffering in loneliness and silence. I have to admit, I'm so confused about this, Lilah."

"About what? You? Me? Death? Life?"

"*Ja*, all of that and more," he admitted. "I was moving along, making the effort, putting on a good front. I got up, ate a quick breakfast, went to work and stayed at work until sundown. Stopped by a café sometimes for a quick meal or made me a steak and potato at home. Then I'd read *The Budget* or the local paper, do some paperwork, read from my Bible and go to bed. It's not a bad life, but it's a life of isolation. These side projects get me through, stop the boredom, but mostly when I'm doing something like this, I work alone and the people who've hired me leave me alone."

"I can do that," she said, turning to leave.

"*Neh*, that's not what I want." Noah shook his head. "That's the problem. After meeting you, I don't know what I want anymore. Except that I like being around you."

"I don't know either," she replied with a shrug that seemed more like a sob. "This is new ground for both of us. But I can tell you this—I understand you. And... I want to be your friend. I don't believe there is anything wrong with being a friend to someone who has been through the same thing I've been through. I think that is the neighborly thing to do, especially since you are working here on my property. I have discussed this with my three daughters and they seem okay with it. Even Sara, as much as she can be okay about anything. She remembers Joshua the most, you see."

He did see. Noah could only nod his head and wonder how the good Lord had plopped him down right here with an intriguing woman, only to realize that neither of them were ready for that next big step. *Gott* knew the next step, so they might have to lean on that and take their time. Could a few days really change a person lost in such a deep grief?

Maybe they should be still and take this slow.

"Friends?" he asked. "Can we do that, Lilah? Can we abide just by being friends?"

"I want to be your friend," she replied. "We've only now started to get to know each other and people are already talking. Friendship can be the end of it, or it can be the first step to whatever happens next."

He slapped his straw hat against his dark pants, then put it back on his head. "You're referring to your well-meaning friends—Team Lilah—but you're also talking about your misguided daughter, the Against Noah Team, who is confused and overly excited about everything these days because she's getting married without her *daed* there to see her do so?"

She laughed at that, but her expression held a hint of melancholy. "I guess I mean all of the above."

"What we need to do is this," he began, glancing toward the big window on her world. "We need to keep being friends and ignore the naysayers and the matchmakers. How about that for now?"

"I'd like that," she said, the shimmer in her eyes giving him hope. "I'd like that a lot." Then she turned toward the gazebo. "I can almost see it now, Noah. The shape, the workmanship, the beauty of that gazebo. I think I'm going to really enjoy it."

Noah could see it now, too, but what he was seeing had nothing to do with what he was building out in the yard.

And it had everything to do with the woman who gazed at his handiwork while she remembered another man and another time.

Could he change all of that and make her happy again?

Lilah walked out the church doors on Sunday and spotted Sara talking to the three friends who'd be a part of her wedding. They wouldn't stand with her like bridesmaids because the bride and groom would be sitting most of the time. But they would be dressed alike and they'd be on hand to help with whatever was needed. She watched as they giggled together and whispered the latest gossip in each other's ears. Friends since their scholar years, the girls reminded her of blooming flowers about to reach for the sky.

She wanted her daughters to be happy, but she missed having them as little girls. Maybe old age was creeping up on her, but she missed those days of innocence and looking toward the future. Other than raising her girls, she had not looked forward very much after Joshua died. Now she could see that she'd only been living in memories that would not change anything. She'd keep her memories, but she needed to move on.

Noah coming into her life had shown her that in a glaring way. Now she thought about her future in a new light. A confusing light of becoming close to another man.

When Noah came around the corner of the church the Amish shared with the Mennonites who also lived or visited in Pinecraft, she had a flash of a future that both scared her and excited her. She'd never noticed him here before.

Had he come for the message or for her?

Your will, Gott, she thought, she hoped, she prayed.

"A pretty group of young *maidals*," Noah said as he moved closer, but not too close. "I wanted to tell you I'll be at your house early tomorrow. I've got the floor nearly done, and then

I'll move on to the crowning glory of your gazebo, the ceiling and the finial top. It won't be long now, Lilah."

"So soon," she said too quickly. "I mean, that's *gut*. That will give us time to plan the setting. We'll use one of Tanner's trucks to get the church benches set up and the food tables in place. Now that will all depend on the gazebo since it will make a nice backdrop when the couple stands."

"I'd be happy to help with setting up the benches and chairs," Noah said. Then he held up a hand. "I'm not fishing for an invitation to the wedding, however."

Lilah hadn't even considered that. "Of course, you're invited. I insist." Did that sound too forward? "As your thankful friend."

"I'd be honored and I mean it when I say I can help with anything you need, Lilah."

"*Denke*."

"I think it will be a lovely wedding," he said, glancing around as people gave them the side-eye.

"I was surprised to see you here today," she said to change the subject.

He chuckled. "I do attend church, Lilah. Except I have to go out of town on jobs a lot."

"I see. But you're here today."

"I am and now that I've found you, this can count as our first outing together, ain't so?"

"You mean together as friends," she pointed out and then blushed. "We didn't arrive together."

"*Neh*, but I can give you a ride home on my snazzy cart." He pointed to a bright red four-seaters golf cart parked under an old live oak. "That'll sure stir the *blabberwauls*, won't it?"

"That will stir up trouble and yes, gossip, no doubt," she said, laughing.

They both looked up as Sara marched toward them. But today, she had a smile on her face. "*Gut daag*, Noah. Mamm, I'll be home later. We're going to Rachel's house to make sure the dresses are pressed and ready."

"They'll be wrinkled again before the wedding," Lilah pointed out. "I can't believe it's less than two weeks now."

Sara bobbed her head. "*Ja*, and I'm getting even more excited. Abram and I had a long talk last night, about a lot of things." She glanced at Noah. "He sings your praises."

Noah opened his mouth to speak, but Carol and Dana walked up, Carol hobbling a bit but walking again at least.

"Can we go home, Mamm?" Dana asked. "We've been invited to a frol and we need to change."

Lilah decided to test the waters. "Noah has offered me a ride home in his cart. I'm sure he wouldn't mind all of us hopping on." And her reputation would stay intact, she hoped.

Sara glanced from her to Noah. "I think that's nice. I'll see you back home."

Then she turned and hurried away, but Lilah saw her glance back, her smile gone. Noah noticed it, too, and gave Lilah an encouraging glance. "One step at a time."

Lilah worried about Sara's mood swings. Why couldn't her daughter talk to her about whatever else was bothering her?

Carol misunderstood. "I'm being careful, don't worry," she said, her head down. "I do not want to sprain my ankle again, so I'll just watch today."

Noah grinned at Lilah and she had to laugh. He had not corrected Carol's assumption. And neither would she.

Lilah got on the seat by Noah and smiled back at her excited daughters. They needed this, too. They needed a man's perspective and authority every now and then. She wanted her girls to grow up strong and self-sufficient, but she also wanted them to be good people and find mates who would love and appreciate them as much as she did.

She silently prayed that Sara would make it

through to her wedding and then maybe settle down as a new wife. A new wife who had too much on her mind to worry about her middle-aged mother.

It was a lovely day for a cart ride, and Lilah intended to enjoy every minute of it. Things got even better when Noah offered to buy them ice cream.

The whole afternoon felt so right, so why did her guilt make her feel as if she'd done something so wrong? Probably because she'd tried so hard to steer clear of growing closer to Noah, but he kept making that a hard goal to keep.

Chapter Nine

Noah enjoyed watching the girls eat their ice cream sundaes while Lilah smiled as she scooped up a spoonful of rocky road, the crunch of chocolate pieces sounding as she chewed.

"Is that *gut*?" he had to ask, his spoon holding a melting dollop of strawberries-and-cream.

"It is so *wunderbar gut*," she exclaimed, her eyes shining with nothing but joy. "I haven't had ice cream in ages."

Noah decided he'd bring her for ice cream more often. The ice cream street truck that was located near the park and the winding creek stayed here all year long. Easy to walk to or drive to on the cart.

While the girls compared their toppings and talked about the frolic they'd be attending later, Noah studied Lilah's face. She was pretty when she smiled big, something she hadn't done much since they'd met. She'd smiled, but those had been simple and tight expressions, as if she'd been hiding her light underneath a basket.

She stopped eating as her gaze met his. "Why are you staring at me?"

"Was I?" he said before popping more ice cream in his mouth. After he'd enjoyed watching as her eyebrows lifted and her chin jutted out, he explained. "You're easy to look at, is all. But I hope I wasn't being intrusive."

"It is rude to stare," she replied, her tone teasing. "But we need to finish up if I'm to get these two home and changed for their afternoon adventures."

"We're going to Sally Glick's house for singing and treats," Dana said, her head bobbing. "Sally's *mamm* always has the best treats—hot dogs and chips, soda and fruit punch—and she lets us make s'mores over the firepit."

Lilah glanced at Carol. "Is that true?"

"With supervision," Carol said, nodding. "S'mores are so *gut*."

"Maybe I need to build you a firepit, too, Lilah," Noah teased. "I could throw that in and give you a fair price for both."

The girls squealed yes while Lilah shook her head. "What did you say earlier? One step at a time."

"Okay." He gave the girls an apologetic twist of a smile. "But one day."

Carol finished her sundae and put the plastic spoon in the paper cup. "*Ja*, after Sara's never-ending wedding plans are done and finished," she said in a snarky voice.

Lilah shot her daughters a surprised expression. "I'm sorry. You two have been a bit neglected lately. Is your sister harassing either of you for help?"

"*Neh*, she refuses to let us help," Dana replied in a huff. "She's afraid we'll mess things up. Like we are *kinder* or something."

Noah hid his smile, only because Lilah looked so dejected. He didn't say anything, but he could tell her mind was back in turmoil again. Parenting sure wasn't what he'd expected it to be. But then, he had not been around a lot of *kinder* or teens.

"Maybe I can find something you can do to help," Lilah said. "And present it to your sister in a way that will make her think she came up with the idea."

"Can you really do that?" Dana asked in awe. "I mean trick Sara. She seems hard to trick."

"It's not really a trick," Lilah said, backtracking. "It's more of her seeing the logic in letting her sisters be a part of one of the most important times in her life. It would be a shame not to point that out to her in a loving way."

"Oh," Carol said, her dark eyes wide with realization. "Like a teacher showing you how to do math, only you come up with the answers."

"*Ja*, like that." Lilah gazed at her daughters, clearly relieved that she wasn't teaching her girls to be deceitful. "Just so."

Noah sat back and smiled at her. She dealt with them in a loving way, but he knew she fretted over them, too.

"You two please take our trash to that big can by the ice cream truck," she told Carol and Dana. "We need to get home."

After they'd done as she'd asked, Noah turned back to her. "You handled that in a *gut* way, Lilah."

She shook her head. "Sometimes, with Sara, that's how you have to make things happen. She thinks she has all the best ideas and she's very stubborn about changing that notion."

"So you talk her into things and let her think she does have the best ideas?"

"Is that bad of me?"

"I think it's quite brilliant of you and I'm guessing many mothers have done the same throughout time." He squinted. "It's like reverse psychology."

"And here I thought I was the only one who knew that secret," she replied, laughing again.

"Now it will be our secret."

He watched as she absorbed that and then

questioned him. "You won't use this against me, will you?"

"Never. But only if you agree to have ice cream with me once a week."

At first, she drew back and then she chuckled. "You drive a hard bargain, but I will do my best to keep that commitment. After this wedding is over."

"I suppose everything is on halt except the gazebo," he replied, reminding himself that finishing that structure should be his main goal for now. He could do that and get on with his life.

But his life had changed the moment he'd looked into Lilah's eyes.

Disappointment colored her gaze. "That is true, but you've done a lot of the hard work already."

"I still have to finish what I started, in more ways than one."

Her eyes filled with understanding and a pretty blush colored her cheeks, but she didn't respond to his comment with words.

They got up and he guided her to the cart. "I enjoyed this," he told her.

She looked down at the pavement. "I did, too. *Denke*."

He took them home, wishing he didn't have to take them home and leave them. But as he waved goodbye, he thought about Janeen and how she'd wanted children so badly. He'd thought he'd failed her, but her sickness had made her too weak to conceive and he'd had no control over it. None at all. Or at least, he kept telling himself that.

He didn't have much control over whatever he was feeling right now either. And as much as he'd enjoyed today, that lack of control made him hesitate to take things any further than ice cream on a Sunday afternoon. He'd leave it at what he'd told Lilah. Ice cream with her and the younger girls. Wishing for a family, maybe this family, was one thing. But making that happen was quite another. Was he ready for that?

Lilah thanked Noah for the ride and went in with the girls. After they changed into older everyday clothes, she walked with them down the street to the Glick's home where a group of preteens had gathered to play volleyball in the backyard.

"Carol, mind your ankle. You don't need to injure your foot again."

"I'm going to watch the game with Greta Parker. She has a broken arm," her daughter replied with a practical acceptance.

"*Gut* idea." After Lilah had visited with some of the women who were chaperoning, she strolled back to her house and went out to look over the gazebo. She'd wanted to be surprised and from the looks of it now, she'd only see it in all its beauty when it was completely done. The bits and pieces of lumber meant nothing to her, but she could see the pretty wagon wheel pattern of the flooring and the strength of the posts Noah had somehow softened with his tools. They were sturdy, but dainty with Victorian style swirls and angles.

She stood back, picturing the wedding here. This new addition would make a striking backdrop. They expected about one hundred people, and that would be most of the neighborhood and a few folks coming in from other places to attend the ceremony and the dinner afterwards. She'd tell Sara the girls would love to polish the church benches. Sara loved a clean, tidy house. She kept her room perfect and didn't like anyone messing with it.

So she should readily agree with that suggestion and the girls would be part of helping. They could also serve in other ways—helping with the food they'd spread out on the back porch underneath wire domes to keep flies away. Even before the wedding, they'd be needed to help make paper flowers and fill bags with cookies to send home with the guests, something Sara had seen in a wedding magazine.

She sat down on the back steps with a notepad and wrote down tasks for Carol and Dana. Sara should have thought of this, but as usual her daughter was single-minded and centered on what she wanted. That trait needed to change once she was married.

Sara and Abram would be expected to visit those who'd helped with the wedding and thank them for their gifts or thank them while visiting if any friends still had gifts to present. It would be a busy time for the newlyweds before life settled down. Would Sara calm down, or would her overly dramatic mind create new problems?

Lilah said a long silent prayer for her family, as she always did when she worked in her garden. She got up to do some work and her right foot hit a loose board. Then she glanced at the porch, really looking at it for the first time in a long time.

"The porch needs to be fixed," she said, her mind whirling. How had she missed that? The whole porch needed a new paint job. She'd had the front porch cleaned and repainted a few months ago, but she'd been so focused on the garden and the food, she'd neglected the very porch where everything would be served in an assembly line, men first, then women and children.

They'd have plenty of spots for everyone to eat. Benches could easily be turned into tables when pushed together. But the porch needed to be sturdy and clean. She'd put colorful plants in each corner—petunias and lilies maybe or some daisies and jars of fresh-smelling rosemary.

She added this task to her list. She'd start first thing in the morning. She'd need to find someone to help repair the loose floorboards. Tanner came to mind, and Ruth's son Nathan did just such work. She'd get in touch with him first and see if he was available. If not, Tanner then.

What about Noah? Her mind seemed to pop that question right into her head.

"*Neh*."

She said that so loud the stray tabby cat that roamed the neighborhood and got well-fed by everyone ran out from under the porch and hissed at her.

"I know, I know, Goldie," Lilah said, her heart racing from the cat sneaking out like that. "He can't be the one to help. He's already here in my head enough these days. That's like asking for trouble, ain't so?"

Goldie gave Lilah one last glance, and seeing no food dish, took off for a better location.

Lilah stood still, stared at her garden and wondered if she'd be able to get through this summer with grace and wisdom.

"I'll pray on that," she called after the departing feline.

Goldie gave her a dismissive cat glare and crawled through the hole under the fence.

Meantime, she needed to do some weeding and keep her flowers watered so they'd keep blooming all summer. They'd use flowers from her garden to spruce up the tables and for the bride to hold while sitting through the sermons. She lifted her nose to the scents of jasmine and gardenias, roses and orange blossoms. *Gott*'s amazing world, right here under her feet and filled with twisting, tempting paths.

Lilah prayed she'd follow the right path. The path He'd created for her.

She'd find someone, anyone except Noah, to repair and paint her porch. Or she'd learn how to do it herself.

But that little voice in the back of her head kept saying, "Just ask the man. Just talk to him. Let him in a little bit more."

She was slowly becoming ready to make that next move. But only after Sara was married to Abram. And even then, Lilah would be careful to guard her heart.

Chapter Ten

Noah got to Lilah's place late Monday morning, only to find Tanner and Nathan there working on her back porch. They both glanced up when he came walking toward them.

"Noah," Nathan Kohr called out, waving. "We could use an extra hand here."

Noah glanced around. When he didn't see Lilah, he walked to the porch. "What's going on here?"

Tanner grinned. "Isn't it obvious? Lilah was in a panic about this porch and asked us if we'd help fix it up for her daughter's upcoming wedding. She's going to whitewash the floors when we're done. And maybe repaint the ceiling in a sky blue."

Noah squelched the disappointment in his heart. He could have easily done this work for Lilah. They'd had such a great time yesterday, but today was a new day. But this showed she still had doubts, so instead of asking him to help, she'd hired others. Fair enough since he had his own doubts. His heart couldn't go through another hurt again, but he would have gladly done this extra work for free. And yet, she had not mentioned it to him in all their time together yesterday.

He'd best remember their pact to be friends and let it go at that.

"Noah?"

He glanced up at Tanner's questioning gaze. "Oh, sorry. I had some work on the subdivision we've got going east of here. Always something. Now I'm behind."

"*Ach, vell*," Tanner replied. "If you help us with this, maybe we can help catch you up on that gazebo everyone is talking about."

Noah looked toward the kitchen. "I don't know about working with you two. Lilah might want me to stay on my side of the yard."

Tanner shot Nathan a speaking glance, then turned back to Noah. "What's up with you and Lilah? Wait, let me think. She's pretty and sweet and available and you're grumpy, jumpy and available. Is that the problem?"

Noah frowned and shook his head. His friends knew him too well. "You got all that from me building a structure in her yard?"

"*Neh*," Tanner continued. "I got all that from

your frown and how you keep checking the window and door. You like her, don't you?"

"Of course I like her," Noah admitted, wishing he could turn around and go home. "She's paying me *gut* money, so I need to get to work."

Nathan shot Noah his own confused glance. "You've never been about the money, so that excuse falls short."

Noah grunted and then let out a breath. "That is true enough. Lilah and I are friends. It's complicated."

"That's another excuse," Nathan replied in a gentle tone. "It's because you're not ready, am I right?"

Tanner stopped measuring and let out a huff. "Hit me with a hammer. I'm sorry, Noah. I should know how you're feeling since I was a widower when I met Eva. We danced around the truth for a long time before I realized she was the best thing that could happen to me. *Gott* sent her just in time."

Noah couldn't argue with that. "So you and Eva are happy. We can all see that. But how did you get over the grief and guilt?"

Tanner wiped his brow with his shirtsleeve. "Well, I finally told her the truth about my first marriage. That alone lightened my soul and made me know she'd be a great mom to Becky, because Eva understood why I'd kept my secrets. Later, after I chased her down and told her I loved her, we prayed and accepted that we could be miserable alone or happy together. It's that simple, but a hard thing to comprehend when you're still reeling over losing someone."

Nathan nodded. "I know that's why my *mamm* has never remarried. It's too painful for some. I don't know that kind of pain, but I remember how I was so scared for Adina when she was in danger, but I had to overcome that and accept that love conquers all. Even a grieving heart."

Noah rubbed his hands together. "Lilah and I are older and we're taking things slow—friendship has to count for something. *Denke* both. You younger fellows sure are full of wisdom."

"*Neh*, we are full of love and good cooking," Nathan quipped. "Having a helpmate makes everything better. You should try it again. Let your heart work hard for you."

"It is working hard," Noah replied. "I can't help you with this work if Lilah frowns on me hovering around all the time."

The back door opened and she stepped out, her dress a light pink, her hair coiled underneath her *kapp* like a golden ribbon.

Lifting her hands, a mock frown on her face, she asked, "What are you three doing standing around?"

Noah saw the humor in her eyes and breathed a sigh of relief. "They are trying to get me to help them, poor misguided men. I'd slow them down."

Lilah put her hands on her hips. "I doubt that. You are the owner and operator of Lantz Seaside Cottages, ain't so?"

"So," Nathan said, pointing a finger at Noah. "He's afraid you'll pay him less for the work he's already doing here."

"I just might," she replied, a twinkle in her green eyes. "But you know, three sets of hands is even better than two. And if you two help him with his work a bit, I'll throw in noon dinner for everyone. I have some fresh Black Forest ham and a loaf of bread just out of the oven. And sliced market-fresh tomatoes from Georgia."

"Georgia tomatoes are tasty," Nathan said, a plea in that statement. "Any Vidalia onions?"

"I might have a few," she replied with a grin. "You all get to work out here and I'll have Sara help me inside."

Sara. That soured Noah's appetite. The young woman would definitely be displeased with him eating another meal here. But he went on with the conversation. "That sounds like a powerful sandwich."

"She's always feeding someone," Tanner said, "and today I'm for certain glad it's me."

Lilah chuckled, her gaze landing on Noah.

"Are you sure, Lilah?"

She nodded at him, a silent message passing through her eyes with the flurry of a willow tree moving gently in the wind. "I am sure. I can't let you three do all this last-minute work without offering you food. And this time, Noah, your sandwich will be man-sized. No more finger sandwiches for you."

After she went inside, his two young friends eyed him. "You'll need to explain about the finger sandwiches, Noah," Tanner said with a wide grin.

Noah shook his head and grabbed a hammer. He hadn't felt this lighthearted in a long time. Lighthearted and a little light-headed. Being friends with Lilah was the nicest thing that could happen to him so he'd do his best to honor that agreement without overstepping. Even if it meant eating more finger sandwiches.

"Sara, I need your help to make sandwiches for our workers," Lilah said as soon as she was back in the kitchen.

Sara stopped scrubbing the oatmeal pot and glanced out the window. "Why is Noah helping with the porch?"

"Because Nathan and Tanner asked him to

help and in return they are going to help him with the gazebo."

She waited a beat to see if Sara would complain.

Sara studied the men laughing and hammering away. "I suppose many hands are better than none at all."

"That's a nice way to put things," Lilah replied. "How did it go with the breakfast shift at the café this morning?"

Sara stopped scrubbing. "Albert is never happy with my work, Mamm. And I try so hard to be pleasant and efficient. It's ruining these last days before I marry. He's already unhappy about me taking a week off for the wedding and the move to Abram's home. He makes fun of our customs and he's not nice to anyone who is a believer."

Lilah had to wonder what Sara wasn't telling her. "Is this man bothering you in an improper way?"

"What? *Neh*," Sara said, her skin flushed. "He's not that type, thankfully. He's just so mean all the time, as if he's got a beef with the whole world." Sara glanced back at the workers on the porch. "He doesn't have the solid foundation of faith like we do."

"Is this why you've been so distraught lately?"

"I'm not distraught. I'm happy and ready to

be married, but I worry so much about everything." She sighed. "And I've been a brat about so much."

"Oh, that," Lilah replied, keeping her tone light and neutral. "You haven't been yourself lately. I think most of us worry too much when we know worry is just wasting a prayer."

"I do pray," Sara said, "but I still worry about you, about my sisters, about being a *gut* wife, about my job. And what if it rains on my wedding day? I keep hearing a hurricane is brewing in the Gulf—the first of the season and early at that."

Lilah pulled Sara away from the sink and turned her around. "If it rains on your wedding day, you dance in the rain, daughter. You embrace the rain and hug your husband. That is the way of life. We look for joy in life. We hold on to our faith. We know it's all in *Gott*'s hands."

"Is that why it seems so easy for you?" Sara asked, a pout forming on her lips. "You just expect *Gott* to take care of everything?"

A shock ran through Lilah. "The Lord does take care of things. What are you talking about?"

"You don't seem to miss Daed as much as I do. How do you smile and laugh or find joy when you've lost the man you loved. How is that possible?"

Lilah pulled away and stared over at Sara. "I miss your father every day, Sara. All the time."

"But you seem to keep going. You always seem at peace, as if you've forgotten when he died. I was old enough to be there and remember watching him waste away. I couldn't understand why his heart wouldn't work probably. I still remember his last words to me. I think about that every day. And late at night when I can't sleep."

Lilah could see her daughter's anxiety went deeper than she'd realized. How could she help Sara see that life didn't stop for anyone and that sometimes you had to make the best of a bad situation? She'd tried so hard to keep her daughters on the straight and narrow while she also allowed them to learn and grow when they did make mistakes. Surely she hadn't failed at being a proper mother. Or maybe Sara couldn't grasp a widow finding happiness again. All these years, Lilah had tried to hide her grief to protect her daughters. She might need to rethink that and explain to them how she really felt most days.

"This is why you frown on Noah and I being friendly, *ja*? Because you don't understand me being happy when you've lost your *daed*?"

Sara nodded, hesitated for a moment, then sighed again. "*Ja*, because I can't understand."

She wiped her hands on a dish towel and leaned against the counter. "I mean—I thought I'd accepted losing him but now that I'm getting married, I just really miss him. That's why I can't grasp you *not* missing him."

"I do miss him," Lilah admitted. "I don't understand death or mourning or how my life changed overnight. I don't understand why you seem to think the worst of me only because a man had paid attention to me. I see that this wedding has brought up your grief, but this has to stop, Sara. You need to go talk to the bishop or one of the ministers because grief is sneaky and can ruin your attitude and make you lash out at others, as you're doing with me these days. You should be able to let go of these constant worries and live your life, while you can."

"And that means, before it's too late?" Sara asked, her eyes misty. "What if I lose Abram, the way you lost Daed. I'd never be able to get out of bed and function."

"You'd be surprised what you have to do when you need to do it," Lilah said in a quiet tone. "I have mourned your father for ten years now and I will always mourn him until I see him again in Heaven. But he would want me to stop that and live my life. I can't bring him back, but I can move forward and honor him by trying my best to do right and to be joyful."

Sara gave her a sad glance. "Does Noah make you feel joy?"

Lilah thought about that for a moment. "He makes me smile and yes, he is a joy to be around. But we've decided we can be friends. Nothing more. He's still in mourning too, even more so than you and I. So neither of us is ready for anything drastic. Not yet anyway."

"But that day might *kumm*," Sara said. "And then, you'll forget Daed altogether."

Lilah didn't want to cry. She blinked back tears and said on a hoarse moan, "That will never happen. And you need to quit making me feel guilty about losing the man I loved. Isn't it enough that you've continued to judge me and remind me of my shortcomings when I hired this man because you wanted this gazebo built? Would it have been better if an older, less handsome man had shown up?"

Sara wiped at her tears and bobbed her head. "*Ja*, it would have been much better. Why does Noah seem so perfect for you, Mamm?"

Chapter Eleven

Lilah got busy with making the sandwiches, Sara falling in behind her without another word. Considering her words with a prayer that she'd chose them wisely, Lilah turned to her eldest and asked, "Do you like Noah or not, because these mood swings and your sour attitude are beginning to worry me."

"You told me *not* to worry," Sara pointed out as she slapped mayonnaise and mustard against fresh bread.

"Sara, I'll remind you to be respectful to me."

Sara lowered her head, her gaze on the men outside. "I do like Noah, Mamm. That's part of the problem. I shouldn't like him. I'm trying to stop something we might all regret."

Lilah let that sink in. Her daughter liked Noah, but—

"But you don't want Noah and I to get any closer because *you* feel guilty?"

Sara turned to Lilah. "So guilty. That's why

I'm waffling between happiness and panic, Mamm. One minute I'm happy for you and him and then next, I want to sit down and cry. Just cry. This is seriously messing up my wedding happiness."

Lilah glanced at her pouting daughter and started laughing.

"Mamm, this is serious. Are you all right?"

"I'm fine, honey," Lilah said. "And so are you."

She took Sara away from her work and placed her hands over her daughter's. "Please stop now. You just accused this—this idea you came up with—of interfering with your wedding plans. You are the only one who seems to feel that way. I'm laughing because even though you've been honest with me, you're still being a bit selfish."

"Selfish?" Sara pulled away and did a twirl of frustration. "I'm not selfish. I just have a lot on my mind and now I have to worry about you and Noah becoming an item."

"We are not an item," Lilah said. "I've explained it over and over. We are friends, and you can either accept that and get on with your plans or you will regret this once you're married and realize how foolish you've been. Please, enjoy these last few days before your wedding, okay? Noah and I are mature adults as I've pointed out to you. And he and I will be friends long after your wedding day. Don't ruin things with worry and guilt. I mean it. If you can't get your head straight, I will tell him to stop working right now and the gazebo will be what it is, as is."

"That would be horrible," Sara said, shaking her head, that hesitation Lilah had seen returning. "I want my wedding to be pretty and special." She took a long breath and looked out at the half-finished structure. "I promise I'll put these silly worries out of my head."

Sara was holding back, and now Lilah had to wonder if this had something to do with Albert and work or an ongoing disagreement with Abram or something more about Lilah and Noah. Something her daughter refused to share. But what could that be?

Deciding they'd only have the same conversation over and over, Lilah pulled back and gave in to truly letting *Gott* help her get through this.

"How about we get back to finishing up these sandwiches and then you and I will take a walk and get some ice cream or lemonade. Just the two of us. We both have a lot of emotions roiling around and that's to be expected with this big change. But don't ruin your new life before you even get started."

"I'm going to try," Sara replied. "It's so hard to let go of Daed, even after all these years."

"I certainly understand that," Lilah said as they put the sandwiches on a big tray and added some fruit and chips. "Let's take care of our helpers and then we'll find some quiet time to talk about whatever you want to discuss."

That calmed Sara down. "Mamm?"

"What?" Lilah asked, hoping Sara would tell her the truth.

Sara opened her mouth to speak, then closed it tight. With a nod, she gave Lilah a weak smile. "Noah is a *gut* man, and he's a nice-looking man. That much I can see for myself."

Then she opened the door with a smile on her face and passed out paper plates to the men before she glanced back at Lilah with a beseeching look in her eyes.

Now Lilah's blood pressure seemed to go sky-high. What was Sara hiding?

"This looks mighty *gut*," Nathan said. "I'll be happy to work on your house anytime, Lilah."

Tanner nodded. "I second that." He grabbed a heavy sandwich and a handful of potato chips. "*Denke*."

"We're going to run an errand," Lilah said, trying to be polite. "And get in some girl time before Carol and Dana return from the park. I'll leave you some ice water in the cooler."

Noah had been quiet but he took his plate and

looked up at Sara. "It's kind of you to help your *mamm* with this, Sara."

Sara gave him a weak smile. "I like to cook and clean," she said. "Mamm taught us to be neat and to always have food on hand."

"Your *mamm* is thoughtful that way," he replied, smiling at Lilah.

Lilah held her breath, but to her credit, Sara passed out food in a prim and polite silence, with a tight smile pasted onto her face. After she'd done her duties, she asked if they needed anything else before pivoting back inside the house.

Soon the men were sitting under the big oak, laughing and talking as they enjoyed their meal, and Lilah and Sara started out toward the town center.

"Do you want to talk more about what we've discussed?" Lilah asked.

"Can we just chat about everyday things? About the wedding. I'm not trying to shift things, but I need a break from Noah and the gazebo discussions."

"So do I," Lilah admitted. "We should drop in on Ruth and see how her quilting frolics are going. I've finished your wedding quilt but I'll give it to you later, of course."

Sara's solemn expression widened to a smile.

"I can't believe I have my own wedding quilt. *Denke*, Mamm."

"It's tradition," Lilah said. "Ruth and her quilters helped me finish it."

"I'd like visiting Ruth's shop," Sara said. "I need some material for new dresses after I become a married woman. I want to look pretty for Abram."

"You are pretty," Lilah told her, all the while praying that they'd finally settled this sticky situation even if Sara still had some concerns. She'd talk to Noah later, too, and explain. "I know you'll be a beautiful bride."

Sara's smile filled with joy. "I think I'm beginning to see the big picture, Mamm."

Lilah took a deep breath and hoped the big picture in her daughter's head was a *gut* one. "Oh, and what does that look like?"

Sara ran her hand over a palm frond as they passed a leaning tree. "You do have a right to be happy and I have been so selfish and mean. How do you stand me?"

"I love you," Lilah replied. "And I know all the feelings circling in your head and your heart. But I can tell you this, Sara. You have a right to be happy, too. Your *daed* loved you girls so much and he'd want you to have the best of life. He's here with us, honey, in our hearts."

Her daughter let out a soft gasp. "I suppose

he would." But she didn't seem so sure. "I'm sorry I've been so wishy-washy. Abram says I have the bride jitters. He's been so understanding, but I fear he'll be fed up with me by the time our wedding day arrives."

"Abram loves you just as your *daed* and I do. You've just got a lot going on in that overthinking head of yours."

Sara nodded and blinked away her tears. "I'm going to find my joy, starting now." Then she turned to Lilah and giggled. "I'm getting married."

"That's more like it," Lilah replied, relief washing over her. She hoped this truce would last. Sara didn't need to be sad right now.

And neither did she.

Noah helped Nathan and Tanner finish changing out the worst of the porch floorboards. He and Tanner did that while Nathan followed with a fresh coat of paint. Once they were finished, he turned toward his looming task.

"We meant what we said," Nathan called after him. "I know you like to do these projects alone, but sometimes it's nice to have a friend to help out. Let us help, Noah."

Noah couldn't argue with that and Nathan's earnest expression. These two were each about fifteen years younger than his forty-seven, but he sure would take either of them as a son.

"I'd like your company," he admitted. "This has been a tough one."

"How so?" Tanner asked as he lifted his tool chest and followed Noah and Nathan across the yard. "This structure looks sound to me."

"It's not the structure," Noah replied. "It's me."

The mid-afternoon sun was bright and the humidity was high, but Noah felt some hope today. Sara had been kind to him, and Lilah had looked as prim and pretty as ever. Now his heart ached even more for something he didn't know how to put into words.

"I am a nuisance to the bride-to-be," he told the two men waiting for him to speak. "Sara wanted this gazebo, but she does not want *me* here."

Nathan shot him a speaking look, then finally started talking. "Because you have eyes for her *mamm*?"

Noah balked at that bold question. Both of his friends had heard his concerns but he needed to make it clear. "Because I like her *mamm*, *ja*. But we are keeping the line drawn between friendship or anything more. It seems everyone but Sara thinks we are a fine match, but we are the ones who will decide if we should be a match. I doubt Lilah can move beyond friendship."

"Nor you?" Tanner asked, because they'd already had a similar conversation and he was probably growing tired of Noah's laments.

"Nor me." Noah started measuring wood for the starburst flooring again. "We're both fairly young still, but I sure feel old watching Lilah with her girls. They are a constant mystery to me."

"Most women are," Nathan replied with a laugh. "But when they leave us *ferhoodled* at times, other times they make our lives *wunderbar gut*."

"I am certainly confused," Noah replied. "I never expected to—"

"—like a woman again?" Nathan and Tanner both finished.

Noah trusted them so he nodded. "*Ja*, I sure do like her."

"Get in line, friend," Tanner said. "When you've been hurt by love, you tend to shy away from love."

"You'd make a *gut* poet," Nathan teased. "But you are correct. I've had to learn a lot over the last year or so," Nathan admitted. "Adina came here to find her sister and we were forced together to find a criminal. Now her sister is back in Pennsylvania and Adina is sad about that.

I've had to learn to let her be sad sometimes, because she loves me and she's happy here, even when she's having a bad, emotional day."

"You make no sense," Noah replied, chuckling. "But you went through a lot to get to where you are now—happily married and smiling all the time."

"He's downright *lecherich* and lovesick," Tanner said, his tone droll. "But then, so am I."

"You?" Nathan teased. "You were always so grumpy and stoic until that ray of sunshine we all call Eva showed up. Now you actually seem happy."

They all laughed at that.

"I don't know what will happen with Lilah," he said after sawing a board. "But I do know I'd like to keep her in my life."

"*Ach*, *vell*," Tanner replied, "building this lovely gazebo in her yard is a *gut* start, I'd think."

"And getting it ready in time for Sara's wedding will win you points, too, I reckon," Nathan added. "So let's get on with it."

Noah's work went fast because he had helpers. They finished the floor just as the sun was beginning to slip down toward the water to the west. The wagon-wheel shape of the floor did a beautiful starburst as the evening sun cast a creamy yellow beam across it.

"Lilah will be thrilled," he told Tanner and Nathan as they cleaned up and put away their tools. "I appreciate the help and the company. Maybe my staunch declaration of wanting to do these projects alone has caved in on me a bit."

"Does that mean you'll need our assistance more now?" Tanner asked with a mock glare of fear. "I'll be in trouble. Eva already complains I work too hard, but she doesn't understand this isn't work to me."

Nathan chuckled. "I always need extra work, especially since I just learned this week I am to be a father."

"Well, you two didn't waste any time," Tanner said, slapping his friend's back. "I'm happy for you."

"So am I," Noah said, that shard of longing still deep inside his heart. "You'll be a *gut* father, Nathan."

Nathan grinned from ear to ear. "Don't repeat that information. I don't want to burst Adina's bubble."

"That's a piece of advice right there," Tanner said. "Never burst a woman's bubble or steal her thunder. That won't go well."

Noah let out a grunt. "I think you might have hit the nail on the head, my friend. I'm doing that to Sara each time I smile at her *mamm*, and that for certain sure does not make the bride happy."

Tanner frowned in protest. "The bride should be glad her *mamm* has been spending time with a *gut*, solid man who'd be a blessing to any woman."

Noah grunted again. "I think I might need to go to the source of my problems and have a talk with her. What advice do you two have on that conversation with Sara?"

Nathan looked at Tanner and they both said the same thing.

"Run away!"

Noah got the impression talking to Sara about their differences might not be the best plan. But he had to start somewhere, or else he might lose the best thing that had happened to him lately.

Being around a true family and a woman he could easily love.

Chapter Twelve

Lilah laughed as Ruth brought out pie and *kaffe*. The quilting circle was in full swing. Several of Ruth's friends, women Lilah knew, were gathered for their weekly quilting frolic held here in the shop.

"I'm so glad you two came by," Ruth said, laughing. Her daughter-in-law Adina chatted with Sara. Those two had become fast friends recently. Adina would be a positive influence on Sara.

"I'm glad we decided to visit, too," Lilah replied. "We needed this break. Martha and Ramona went over the menu with us again when we checked in with her—she's added celery soup and a lot of pretty celery decorations, of course."

Sara chimed in. "Because we will need all the prosperity and fertility we can get." Then she blushed prettily. "I mean when the time comes."

Adina lifted her head from her stitching, her

gaze zooming in on Ruth. "Is that why you fed me celery at my wedding and almost every day since?"

"It worked, didn't it?" Ruth asked with a proud smile.

Lilah glanced from Ruth to Adina. "You're glowing," she said to Adina.

"I'm going to have a *bobbeli*," Adina blurted out, tears in her eyes. "And now I find out celery had something to do with it. My *aenti* back home never told me about such things."

They all began to congratulate her and hug her while she grinned and poked at Ruth. "Celery. I mean we didn't get to go to many weddings, but I do remember when Blythe got married, there were several celery dishes. I don't even like celery."

They all cackled again at that, making her blush even more.

Lilah glanced at Sara. She laughed and touched Adina on the arm, smiling at her friend.

"I'm so happy for you," Sara told Adina. "Mamm, more celery, please."

They settled back, smiling and joking over peach pie and their tea and *kaffe*. Ice cream was always a treat but stopping here had been exactly what they both needed.

Then Ruth's friend Ellen turned to Lilah.

"And now you can tell us about these rumors we've been hearing."

"What rumors?" Lilah asked, forgetting for a moment that the grapevine here was strong and sturdy and always busy.

"We hear you and Noah Lantz have been seen together," Ellen continued. "Are you walking out with a man, Lilah?"

Lilah blushed now, right along with her daughter.

"Tell them, Mamm," Sara said, her smile not as strong now. "Tell them you're just friends."

"That is the truth," Lilah finally replied, finding her voice again. "He's a nice man who is doing some work in my garden. So we have gotten to know each other. But he'll be done with the gazebo in time for the wedding and maybe after that, my life can go back to normal."

Sara lifted her dark eyebrows. "We've all been a bit on edge with the wedding plans. I asked Noah to build the gazebo because Abram knows him and recommended him. I never dreamed he and Mamm would become fast friends, however."

Ruth studied both mother and daughter, then shrugged. "I think it's a great match."

"So do I," Ellen said as if waiting for a rebuttal.

Soon the other women all nodded. "You could do worse."

Lilah gritted her teeth while she held her smile. "We are only friends."

Sara went quiet, but she did smile at Lilah. "Or so they both keep saying."

Lilah had a feeling these rumors would only get worse and that might add more fuel to her eldest daughter's bad attitude.

Noah returned to Lilah's house on Tuesday afternoon. He'd done the rounds on the two developments his crew continued to work on, but the radio weatherman mentioned that possible early hurricane out in the Gulf, so he'd also gone over preparations for that with them. The whole state was holding its breath, hoping the storm would fizzle out or turn back to the water and disappear back into the deep sea. The wedding was the last Saturday of May. At the end of next week to be exact.

Most people involved in construction watched the weather with a keen eye on a *gut* day. But a hurricane could take down a brand-new housing development. While he had insurance, storm damage could put everything on hold. He'd stop to help those in need, of course. He and his crew were more than willing to do that. But restarting a new build when you were almost finished with it was hard work and only delayed things even more.

He had twelve days to finish this piece. The storm could take its time deciding if it wanted to veer back out into the Gulf. They'd know more about that as the days went by. All the more reason to get this finished. These storms could change course overnight.

Now that he had the floor done, he could move on to the roof. He'd build it piece by piece, starting with the frame.

Nathan and Tanner said they'd come back at the end of this week to lay thick red bricks around the gazebo as a walkway and a decorative touch for dish gardens and potted plants. Lilah could make a flower bed around the bricks if she wanted.

He planned to explain it to her today.

He began his work in the quiet, the scents of jasmine, gardenia and wisteria tickling at his nose. This garden always smelled like a bouquet. A hint of roses mixed with magnolias and lilies. He felt such a sense of peace here.

A couple of hours and several measured boards later, he heard someone call out, "Hi."

He turned from where he'd laid the ceiling beams to see Lilah walking toward him with a glass of iced tea with lemon.

"Howdy," he called, putting his measuring

pencil behind one ear, safe underneath his summer hat. "That looks mighty refreshing."

She handed him the tea and nodded. "Could we talk for a minute?"

"I'll have more than a minute if you don't mind me taking a break. It's sure turning to high summer around here."

"I know," she said. "I hope the old oaks and pines will keep us cool on the day of the wedding."

"You have *gut* shade here," he said as they moved toward two old outdoor chairs just off the porch. He wondered if she'd heard about the possible storms.

But he didn't get to ask her that.

Once they were settled, she turned to him. "Sara is doing better. We had a good visit when we walked to town the other day. Went by Ramona's place to finish up on the wedding menu and then visited Ruth's quilt shop."

"That sounds like a nice time."

"It was. Sara admitted something to me and I wanted you to know about it."

"Okay," he said, bracing himself, the condensation on his glass cooling his sweaty palm.

"She likes you, Noah, but she doesn't want to like you."

Noah took that in while he sipped on his sweet tea. Then he sat his half-full glass down on the soft grass. "That sounds just about like how her *mamm* feels about me, too."

Lilah's face filled with shock and a bit of embarrassment. "I reckon you're right about that."

"I have to admit—people either like me or they don't. But I've never had someone like me but not want to like me. How can I fix this?"

She laughed and pushed at her *kapp* ribbons. "Not with a hammer and nails, I can tell you that." Then she turned serious. "I don't know that it's fixable. I loved my husband so much and Sara loved her *daed.* She's missing him badly now, of course, and I believe your presence here has caused her to see that I'm a mature woman who might get lonely now and then. She can't accept that because it would be like a betrayal to my husband, but she's trying. She says she'll be polite so she won't ruin her own wedding but I can tell she's still holding something back."

Noah thought about that, then said, "So she blames herself for getting me here in the first place? The guilt of putting you and I together has made her lash out?"

"*Ja*, that's it exactly," Lilah replied. "It's not logical but she wishes she'd never asked for the gazebo to be built. It's too painful to move on."

"I certainly understand that feeling," he said. "But Lilah, we can be friends. I don't want to rush things here and neither do you. That guilt you've both experienced is here in my heart, too. We can go over this a hundred ways, but we are not doing anything wrong. We are friends. New friends who've been in the same community but never in the same close vicinity of each other until now." He picked up his glass again and took another long sip of the freshly brewed tea. "That's *Gott*'s timing, Lilah, not ours."

"You think so?" she asked, her question like a low whisper moving over his ears. He thought he heard a hint of hope in there somewhere.

"I believe so. I go to church and I've seen you there, but I never once thought of approaching you. Now I'm here most every day and well, my whole attitude has changed. I've changed over this last week or so. And it's because when I walked through your gate, it was as if I'd walked through a dark curtain and found the light again. I find peace here and I want what I'm building for you to bring you peace. Not pain or sorrow or regret, Lilah. But peace. A peace beyond understanding."

She gave him a look he'd remember forever. A look of longing and hope and weariness all wrapped up in a soft smile. "I'm glad my garden brings you that kind of peace, Noah."

"But—"

"But I don't know if we can keep this up after you're finished with your work here."

"I thought we'd have even more time to visit after the wedding," he replied. "As friends."

"We will have to see about that," she said, rising. "I wanted you to know if I seem distant or even rude, I have to consider my children—my girls—for now. This wedding is a big event and I won't make Sara sad in any way."

He stood, too. "I understand. I'd better get cleaned up and get on home."

They were walking back toward the house when the back door opened. Carol and Dana ran out to them.

"What's wrong?" Lilah asked, fear in her question.

"Sara is having one of her meltdowns," Carol explained. "She just learned more about the hurricane building in the Gulf and she's hearing it might hit the week of her wedding."

Dana shrugged. "And right now, she's the one being a hurricane. She is whirling in a tizzy in her bedroom."

Noah wanted to say so many things but he knew it wasn't his place to go in and tell a grown woman to stop being so dramatic and selfish. He'd never known how to raise a child so maybe this kind of thing was normal.

"I have to go," Lilah said, her voice apologetic. "I will see you tomorrow, *ja*?"

"I'll be here," he replied. "I hope things can calm down again."

"So do I," Lilah said as she hurried away.

Noah stood there as the last of the sunset glistened like a beacon out over the yard. The golden hour for nature.

Their peace had been broken, but Noah knew he'd be back here in this garden again. And he'd keep coming back long after the bride-to-be had gotten over her tizzy fit.

Chapter Thirteen

The next day, the smell of fresh wood permeated the yard, its sweet scent mixing with that of a thousand blossoms. The warm summer day now slumbered and shifted away from the sound of hammering and sawing, and the lull of bees buzzing and butterflies fluttering. The gloaming sparkled against the blanket of the coming night, the last of the sun's rays spreading wide across the sky.

Lilah sipped her chamomile-and-mint tea and glanced around, trying to picture the wedding in her mind. Would they have sunshine or rain and wind? Ten days left to find out.

Sara was calmer now, because Lilah and her two sisters had reminded her earlier that *Gott* would be in control on the day of her wedding. Even Sara couldn't argue with that.

"It's about Abram and you," Lilah told her. "If we have to bring everything inside and eat out of paper plates, it will always be about the love you two share."

"I don't want a storm to *kumm*," Sara kept saying. "We've planned and worked and calculated, and now that the time is near, it might all be ruined."

"It's out of your control," Carol, ever pragmatic, told her. "You're borrowing worry, and no amount of calculating can stop nature's ways. We all know that."

Dana patted Sara's arm. "We can stand as a group on the porch and the rain will be like music." She shrugged. "It'll be tight on there with so many, but we'll make do."

"Not if we get blown away," Sara said on a sniff. Then she wiped her eyes and nodded. "Am I being a brat?"

"*Ja*," both of her sisters said.

Sara frowned. "I didn't mean for you to agree with me."

"Then don't ask such questions," Carol retorted.

"I pity the man who marries you," Sara shot back.

"I'm pitying Abram right now," Carol replied.

"I'll take care of my husband and you know I love him. I can't wait to be on my own with him." Sara glanced at Lilah for backup.

"Enough," Lilah told them before a brawl

broke out. "No one needs pity here. But we do need to trust in *Gott* and continue on with our plans. With a backup plan if needed."

"We can't control everything," Dana added, her words kind and sure. "But we can control our attitudes, ain't so? Daed used to tell us that."

"You're too young to remember," Sara said, her voice kind now. But Lilah saw that faraway trace of a secret in her daughter's eyes. "But I know Mamm has repeated it to us over and over."

"That's correct. And Dana has heard it even if she doesn't remember it. Now we have much to do and we'll keep on. It will all work out, one way or another."

Then she turned to Sara. "While we're all here, I'd like the girls to get more involved with your wedding."

"How so?" Sara asked, her tone firm.

"I thought you might have some ideas," Lilah prompted, waiting.

"We can do things," Dana replied. "Fold napkins, iron tablecloths or help decorate."

"I can run errands for you on my bike now that my ankle is completely healed," Carol offered.

Sara looked flabbergasted at first, but when Lilah shot her a warning glance, she took the hint. "You know, Samantha has offered to make paper flowers for the tables. You two could help with that, for certain sure."

"I love making paper flowers," Dana said. "We'll get that done quick."

"I'll let Samantha know," Lilah said, nodding her approval. "Since she's right next door, you can call out for me if you need anything."

Sara smiled and stood up, proud of her generosity, from the smugness in that smile. "And you'll both come in handy with serving the food. Your kitchen manners are impressive. *Ja*, please plan on helping to serve punch and cake along with my friends Missy, Laurel and Marilyn. I'd appreciate that." Then her eyes lit up. "They are wearing light pink dresses. You two can wear your new mint dresses to complement them."

"They'll match the flamingos we saw at the zoo that time," Carol said, clapping. "And we'll match the mints Ramona and Martha are making as gifts to the wedding guests."

"That sounds perfect," Sara replied, pleased with herself.

Lilah had to hide her own smug smile, so she'd sent them all to the kitchen to help her with supper. And the whole while she wished she could have invited Noah to stay, but that would only have added fuel to the fire with Sara.

After they'd eaten and cleaned up in the

kitchen and the girls had gone to their rooms, Lilah headed into the living room and pulled out her Bible. She loved reading here in the quiet with just one lamp burning. She had her herbal tea and an almond cookie on the small table beside her old worn floral-embossed chair. At times like this she missed Joshua so much her heart would burn and her breath would leave her body. He used to sit in the blue chair across from her and read *The Budget* or some type of farming magazine. Even though they'd always lived here in town, Joshua had done some work for one of the orange growers who had groves out from the city and he'd made a fair salary doing that along with his work at the produce markets.

Her husband had a hand in making her yard so pretty. He'd planted orange and lemon trees along the fence lines. The smell of orange blossoms also mixed with the other scents during the spring.

Now, silence filled her heart and head and she asked *Gott* to show her the way, to give Sara a new heart that didn't center so much on herself, to bring Carol and Dana strong husbands but also to fill them both with strength to make their own way in the world.

When she heard thunder far away, she thought about the storm brewing out there across the

Gulf. Florida had little pop-up rain showers all summer long, but a hurricane was another matter altogether. She'd learned a lot about hurricanes living in the Sunshine State. These storms were not to be ignored, wedding or no wedding. But she would prepare accordingly.

She got up and found a pen and paper and made her Plan B list. Sara came walking up the hallway.

"I can't sleep."

"Me either," Lilah admitted. "I was about to make a list—for our Plan B."

Sara looked skeptical. "Do we have one yet?"

"*Neh*, but you can help me—it's your wedding after all."

Sara nodded. "I'll make a cup of that tea. You're right, Mamm. I want to be married much more than I want a nice wedding." Then she pivoted halfway to the kitchen. "I want both, actually," she admitted. "And maybe that's where I need to learn a lesson."

After Sara walked away, Lilah shook her head and lifted her hands to the sky. "I will never understand this child's mood, Lord."

And she'd never considered that losing a spouse wasn't just hard on the other spouse. It affected children, too. Lilah had protected her eldest daughter, thinking to spare Sara any grief, but they hadn't sat down and actually talked much about Joshua's passing, except in simple terms. It might be time to dig deeper into this sad situation. She would pray for her daughter to get through all her anxieties. And she'd urge Sara to talk to someone with more wisdom that Lilah.

Sara left early the next morning, first to go to work and then to talk to Ramona about last-minute menu changes if the weather turned bad. If they got rain, that could be manageable. But a full-on storm would change everything.

Lilah hoped Ramona would calm Sara down the way she'd calmed many a bride. Ramona was like a ray of sunshine, who never had any bad thoughts in her head. That might help, especially since she was a neutral person—not a family member.

Sara had told Lilah that after she finished at Ramona's place, Abram was picking her up for their next session with the bishop. She wouldn't be home until late since she and Abram had been invited to supper with the bishop and his wife.

Now Lilah stood watching Noah work. As discussed the night before, after they got home from school, the girls had gone next door to make paper flowers to place on all the tables they'd have across the yard for the wedding dinner. Samantha had been delighted to have some busy hands to help, and the girls could visit with her younger daughter, Katherine, while there. So another task off the list.

They'd help add freshly trimmed and cleaned celery plants in glass jars to the mix the day of the wedding. Sara's suggestion this morning. Lilah had made it a point to thank her for letting her sisters do small tasks here and there.

That left Lilah standing here, daydreaming, when she should be freshening tablecloths and folding the new linen napkins she'd washed to soften them. Ramona had loaned her a whole box of cloth napkins of various colors, but Lilah had made the mint green ones for the bride-and-groom table. Sara could keep them after the wedding was over.

Lilah let out a sigh and started back on her folding. But her gaze kept going back to Noah. He'd finished the floor and he'd started putting in the ceiling panels. Nathan showed up to help, making her feel better. Being here alone with Noah made her feel exposed and…well…he was too tempting. She wanted to go out and watch him work, talk to him, hand him a hammer.

Be a helpmate.

Whoa. That sure came up as quickly as a pop-up rain shower.

But the more she thought about it, the more

she had an image of them working together as a team. Only she'd told him she needed to keep her distance for now. And she would.

"I need to stop staring out the window and focus on my work," she told herself.

So she did that by moving away from the window. She put the napkins in a neat pile on the mudroom shelf, scrubbed the kitchen floor, then fixed meat loaf for supper to go along with fresh field peas and corn bread, with mashed potatoes on the side. She had fresh strawberries and shortcake for dessert.

When she'd finished a few hours later, Carol came running in. "Mamm, can we stay at Samantha's house a little longer. Katherine wants us to play a new game her *grossmammi* gave her for her birthday. It's a board game and Samantha has approved it and she's making us peanut butter and marshmallow sandwiches for supper with a fruit salad on the side. She says it's too hot to cook real food."

Lilah looked at the big meal she'd made, thinking about how the oven had heated up her kitchen. She'd have to eat alone and have leftovers tomorrow. "That's fine, but don't be a bother and get home by eight-thirty."

"We will," Carol said, dancing back toward the front door. Then she turned again. "Samantha says I'm old enough to babysit now and

Katherine wants me as her sitter. I can make my own money."

"That's *wunderbar gut*, sweetheart."

Lilah loved how Carol's face lit up. Her middle daughter had a sweet disposition. Dana was her shy baby. And Sara, well, Sara was her fluttering butterfly, ever-changing and always surprising.

Lilah stood still in her quiet kitchen, sunrays shimmering across the dining table like a soft beacon. The big, lonely dining table.

So, despite her plan to avoid him until after the wedding, Lilah decided she'd invite Noah to supper. She had plenty and no one would be here to condemn her with sour stares.

Having made that decision, she fixed a pitcher of ice water with lemon and orange slices in it and got two plastic cups she kept on hand for the girls and their friends and went outside to the porch to offer Nathan and Noah a drink.

When Noah glanced over and saw her, he smiled and Lilah knew she was done for. She had a huge crush on the man building her gazebo. And she wasn't sure she could avoid him when he would be here for the rest of this week and part of next week. That wasn't a long time, but trying to stay away from him would make it seem like months not days.

"Hello," he called as she held up the water pitcher. "Is that for us?"

"*Ja*." She motioned them to the porch. "I know you have a water jug, but this is fruit water. It's better."

Nathan chuckled. "Don't have to call me twice. It sounds refreshing."

"It sure does," Noah replied as they made it to the porch steps, both taking a seat on the wide wooden planks. "We won't *kumm* any farther," he said. "We're dirty and sweaty."

Lilah was well-aware of the sheen of sweat on his brow. She suddenly became nervous and almost dropped the pitcher. Noah caught it and steadied her.

"I think you need some of this, too. Are you dehydrated?"

"Something like that," she replied, her throat dry, her pulse beating like a pelican flying across the cresting waves of the ocean. "I haven't had much water today."

Nathan took it all in as he gulped down his cupful, his gaze moving from Noah to Lilah. "Uh, I need to head home. I can come back tomorrow afternoon, Noah."

"*Ja*, sure," Noah said, his smile on Lilah. He took a sip of the water she'd handed him. "That's fine."

Nathan shook his head and chuckled again.

"*Denke*, Lilah. I'm going to tell Eva to make me some of this fancy fruit water. If it'll make me grin the way Noah is grinning now, she'll be right pleased with herself."

"You're *welkom*," Lilah said, smiling back at Noah after she'd sent Nathan a fleeting nod. "Just tell her to throw some fresh-cut fruit into a pitcher of ice water."

"Got it," Nathan said. "Well, good night."

With that he left in a hurry. Which left her alone with Noah. Maybe this was a bad idea. She should tell him to have a nice evening. At home alone. Same as her.

But her next words didn't come out that way.

"Would you like to stay for supper then?" she asked before she lost her gumption.

"Should I?" he asked her. "I mean, aren't we supposed to be staying away from each other."

"We were. I mean, we are, supposed to be doing that, *ja*."

"But?"

"I have all this food and it would be a shame not to share it. Unless you have other plans."

Noah laughed out loud. "Lilah, I haven't had other plans in a long, long time. I'd love to have supper with you."

She let go of the breath she'd been holding. "Okay then. You can wash up with the water hose and then just *kumm* in the kitchen. We'll eat by the open windows and use the ceiling fan. I have plenty of food."

"So you've said," he replied. "I have to admit I am hungry. *Denke* for thinking of me."

She didn't tell him that thinking of him seemed to be her new way to pass the time. It occurred to her that she'd be doing that very thing long after he was gone.

But from what she could tell by the joy in his eyes and the amazed expression on his handsome face, she had a feeling he knew that already.

Chapter Fourteen

Noah was on a second helping of meat loaf and potatoes when he stopped and laughed at something Lilah had said. She had the nicest lyrical voice, soft and simple and pure. Right now, she sat regaling him with stories of the stray cat that hovered around her yard waiting for her to feed it.

"Goldie ran off with a chicken wing," she finished. "That cat can scoot away before you know he's nabbed your food."

"Goldie is for sure blessed to have so many people feeding him," Noah said. "He's so big and fluffy, I doubt I could pick him up."

She smiled and sipped her tea. "If he'd even let you pick him up. He's still wild but I have managed to get him up onto the porch so I can pet him."

"Oh, I see. You bribed him with food, same way you got me in here?"

Her smile died and her cheeks flushed pink.

"Is that what you think? That I'd bribe a man with food?"

Seeing her embarrassment, he held up a hand and shook his head. "I was only teasing and it didn't come out right."

She stared at him, then looked toward the front door.

"You're worried, aren't you?" he asked, knowing she was. He should leave—and now. He didn't like sneaking around like a criminal when they were both innocent of anything improper.

"Worried? About what?"

"Lilah, it's plain as day. You only invited me to stay because your daughters aren't here. Especially your oldest daughter."

"That's not—" She stopped and looked down at her plate. "*Ja*, that's what I did. Exactly." Then she got up and started clearing the table. "I'll get dessert."

Noah stood and placed his white cotton napkin on the table. "I think I should go."

Lilah stopped halfway over to the sink, plates in her hands. "You told me you liked strawberry shortcake."

"I do, but I don't like sneakiness and pity."

"I haven't sneaked," she said, her green eyes edged with fire. "And I certainly don't pity you, nor do I feel pitiful. I was alone with all this food."

"And I was here."

"Is there something wrong with asking someone to share a meal with me?"

"*Neh*, not at all," he replied, thinking he should have stayed calm and let it go. But he couldn't, because he cared about her more than he wanted to admit. "What is wrong is that you're too worried and embarrassed about your feelings to share me with your family. I love having meals with you and I enjoyed that first time we all ate together, but until you're sure about you and I being seen together, I'd rather not. *Denke* and now I'll be going."

"But Noah—"

The front door opened and Sara walked in, followed by her two sisters. "Look who I found coming up the sidewalk," she said before she saw Noah there.

"Noah," Carol called. "It's *gut* to see you."

Sara lifted her head, her chin up. "What's this?"

"Supper," Lilah said. "I had all this food and no one to eat it."

"So you invited Noah, of course," Sara said with a calm that didn't reach her eyes.

"And I enjoyed it," Noah replied, glancing at Lilah, regret in his heart. "But now I must leave."

Sara didn't move as he walked by. Carol smiled at him and Dana told him good night.

But Sara—Noah knew he'd run out of there like a coward, but he did feel sorry for Lilah. Sara would probably explain her disappointment and disapproval to her mother.

Like he'd just explained his concerns to Lilah. He was the one being sneaky now. But he couldn't stand up to a grown woman and her daughter and tell them his real feelings. That would end things between Lilah and him forever.

Now he wished he'd left earlier. Before he realized he liked being at the table with her. Before he realized just how lonely he'd been. Before he realized she had only invited him because she was alone.

That should have been a fair reason. Maybe she wanted to be alone with him. *Neh*, she didn't want to be alone at her table but she didn't want to be seen with him. By her children. Or out in the world.

He would stick to the yard from now on.

Lilah busied herself cleaning the kitchen.

"I have strawberry shortcake," she said to anyone who might be listening. Why hadn't she just eaten alone after all? Now Noah was upset, and she felt certain Sara would have something to say despite her attempts to let this issue go.

"I want some," Carol called out. "We had some chips and cookies earlier, but I'm still hungry."

"Me, too," Dana said as she whirled by like a fluttering ladybug. "Samantha had store-bought cookies. I don't think she likes to cook."

"And you, Sara?" Lilah said, testing the waters. "Would you like to sit down with us and have some dessert?"

"I had German chocolate cake at the bishop's house. I'm tired so I'm going to bed."

Lilah glanced up at her daughter. "I know what you're thinking."

"I'm trying not to think," Sara replied. "It's fine, Mamm. I hate to see you eating alone, so I'm okay. Really. Noah seems harmless enough."

Surprised yet again, Lilah went back to fixing dessert. "Did everything go okay with the bishop?"

"*Ja*, we're all set." Sara gave her one more glance that held a thousand unspoken words. "Good night, Mamm."

Lilah watched her daughter walking away, memories of happy times dancing through her mind. Sara used to always want to sit at the kitchen table after she'd been out, to tell Lilah all about a frolic or a gathering to play volleyball in the park. They'd laugh and gossip and sip lemonade or hot tea, have a cookie or a piece of chocolate. Sara had always been moody but not like this.

Her daughter disapproved of her these days and that broke Lilah's heart. Would the other two follow suit and turn on her, too? It wasn't so much that Sara was acting out—that was obvious. But it was how she seemed to be mad all the time, resentful and fuming about something. That wasn't like her, no matter how selfish she seemed at times. Lilah wanted badly to ask Sara what she was holding inside. But she couldn't bring herself to do that.

Now Lilah had to wonder if her daughter wasn't so much worried about her *mamm* with another man, but maybe more worried about her own marriage and how that would change her life completely.

Lilah sat with Dana and Carol and laughed at their stories from next door and how they planned to take turns helping Samantha with her younger children. Their sweet faces helped settle her concerns and remind her that they needed her, too.

"We like them," Carol said. "They are sweet and well-behaved but she needs someone to keep them corralled. Her husband works out of town a lot."

"I'm sure they'll always be sweet and well-behaved," Lilah said, trying to hide her sarcasm. For the most part, her daughters were well-behaved but maybe she'd indulged them a bit too much.

"Why do you look so sad, Mamm?" Dana asked, her big eyes so like her father's. "Did you enjoy supper with Noah?"

"I did enjoy my guest," she admitted. Too much. "But I've had a long day and I'm tired. I cooked but I had no one to share my meal with."

"So you asked Noah," Carol said, giving her a puzzled glance. "Are you two…walking out together?"

Lilah almost burst into laughter. "Do old people do that?" she asked to stall. "Walk out like teenagers?"

"I don't know what you'd call it at your age," Carol replied with look of distaste. "But are you two getting to know each other a lot more?"

"We are friends," Lilah said, thinking she should have that response painted on her head. "He's a nice person and we are the same age, and we have both lost someone we love."

"You have a lot in common, for certain sure," Dana said as she dug into the whipped cream on her shortcake. "And he's not a bad-looking man."

Lilah did laugh at that. "You two are so funny.

Would it be so bad if Noah and I become more than friends?"

"I don't mind," Carol said, one elbow on the table. "You deserve someone nice in your life." She shrugged. "I mean, if Daed can't be here."

Dana chewed on a strawberry. "I never thought about it. That you might be lonely or want to remarry. Having a meal with him isn't that big of a deal. I'm sorry we weren't here to keep you company." She stopped and glanced at Lilah. "But Noah was here and you were kind to think of him. Neither of you had to be lonely. There really is nothing wrong with that, right?"

"Nothing that I can think of," Lilah replied as she started cleaning up the table. She had to blink back the tears her sweet daughter's comments had brought on. "Help me with these dishes and then you two need to go to bed."

"It's been a busy day." Dana yawned and carried plates to the counter. "I'll cover the rest of the meat loaf. We can have meat loaf sandwiches for dinner tomorrow."

"I like that idea," Lilah said. Then she turned to where the gazebo sat, dark and unfamiliar, in her yard. As unfamiliar as having Noah in her yard.

That gazebo had been built to last a long time. It would probably take her that long to forget the man who built it. A few weeks ago, she couldn't have imagined how her life, her mindset, would be changed by one of her daughter's impulsive notions. *Gott* truly did work in mysterious ways sometimes.

She wondered how Noah would act around her from now on. They had such a nice time until he'd misread her reason for inviting him to supper.

It wasn't that she didn't want to be seen with him or she didn't want others to be around when she was with him. She certainly wasn't ashamed or embarrassed about that but she had been concerned about how her girls would react.

Her intentions, however, had been purely selfish.

She had wanted to be alone with him, but not for the reasons he'd assumed. *Neh*, she had really wanted to be around Noah Lantz—all to herself—so they could have some quiet moments without interruptions or judgment. And that might be wrong for so many reasons, assumed or not.

Sara came down to breakfast the next day with a worried expression and her teeth catching on her lower lip. "Abram says the storm is coming our way and it might turn into a Category Two hurricane before it hits land somewhere along the coast."

Lilah hadn't slept well and hearing this news only added to her own concerns. "We have a Plan B, okay. That's all we can hope for right now. A lot of rain and wind and that it moves through quickly."

"But what if we have to cancel? Think of the ruined foods and all the people coming who might get caught in a storm."

Lilah put a hand on her daughter's shoulder. "If the power goes out we will distribute the food before it ruins and if people get stuck here, we will provide shelter for them all around the neighborhood or we'll all go to the main shelter at the convention center together."

"I surely don't want to be married in a storm shelter," Sara replied. "I suppose I'm borrowing trouble, but it could change everything."

"Except your love for Abram and his for you," Lilah replied. "You'd have a big congregation gathered there to witness your marriage."

Sara smiled at that. "You always manage to look at the bright side, Mamm."

"I suppose I do," Lilah replied. "Is that so bad?"

Sara poured some coffee from the percolator. "*Neh*, but we both know things don't always turn out right. Life can change so quickly. Sometimes, it's hard to keep a promise or make needed changes."

Lilah put some toast and apple butter out onto the small kitchen table. "Sara, are you afraid to get married because we lost Daed at such a young age?"

Sara flinched at that question. "Of course not." Then she grabbed a piece of toast and headed back toward her room. "I have to work the morning shift. Then I'll finally be able to take some time off and get myself together. So I'll be around more than normal."

Lilah watched Sara scurrying away from her questions and from questions Sara wanted to ask her. But she was beginning to see she'd touched a nerve with that particular question.

Had her husband's untimely death put a fear of loving another in Sara's head? Lilah knew her daughter loved Abram—had loved him since they were *kinder*. But was she afraid of that love and all that marriage brought with it?

So many doubts and still that nagging feeling that something was driving her daughter to these moods and outbursts.

She prayed over and over, asking *Gott* to let this wedding take place and to please help her suffering daughter.

Lilah found her worn Bible and went out on the back porch to read some calming passages. But each time she glanced at the gazebo shining so bright in the morning light she felt a knot in her stomach. Noah Lantz had become a thorn in her side, an aching thorn that pierced her with longing and also split her with doubt and grief. She'd told herself over and over that she'd stay away from Noah until the wedding had taken place, and what had she gone and done instead? Invited him to supper.

No wonder Sara stayed confused. Lilah was sending mixed signals to everyone. It had to stop for the next week or so at least. And maybe even beyond that. She could easily fall for Noah but would that bring her joy or heartache? She was the one afraid to love again. And in an unconscious way, by burying her feelings right along with her husband, she'd put a shield around her children, too. Sara obviously felt that shield and was now trying to break through it and become her own person. But how could she do that with all this angst and guilt clouding her judgment? Lilah decided she'd go and talk to the bishop herself. He could give her some clarity.

Help me to show her the proper path, Lord. Help me to guide my girls without their daed *here to give them wisdom.* Lilah prayed silently until she heard a motor rumbling in the front yard.

Then she got up and hurried back inside the house.

Chapter Fifteen

Lilah didn't see Noah at church on that Sunday, which was probably for the best. When Betty Troyer invited her and the girls over for supper on Tuesday, stating that Abram and Sara would be there, she readily agreed.

Her house was ready for the barrage of people who'd be arriving early next Saturday morning. They had secured a four-seater cart to bring people from the public parking lot up the road to her house. Plenty of room in the backyard for a wedding, but no room for parking out front and the locals frowned at too many automobiles or carts on the street. Most of her friends would either walk or drive their own carts to the parking lot, or take the cart she'd rented for the day. The few out-of-town relatives had booked condos or hotel rooms and would come and go as needed.

Ramona kept her posted on the food, stating that if the storm hit, they'd have generators and they'd pass meals out to whoever happened to be in need. Between Lilah's home and Ramona's big kitchen up the road, they'd make it work with the food, storm or no storm. The food would have to travel via carts, too, but they could cover it with tarps.

All the gifts and some furniture had been moved from Sara's room here to the new house.

That left the garden and the gazebo. Next week, she'd prune and weed the entire yard. The young Amish boy who mowed around all her paths and flower beds would be there to help.

But about that gazebo.

She glanced out now, knowing Noah wouldn't be here on a Sunday afternoon. A perfect time for her to have a quiet moment out there before supper. Carol and Dana were at a youth frolic on the beach, and Sara was with Abram at the new house. Lilah planned to tour it later in the week since it was next to Abram's parents.

Smiling about gaining a whole new family, Lilah looked forward to meeting Abram's three siblings—two older brothers who ran a business together and lived in another town nearby and one sister who had married and moved to Georgia.

"How can I be lonely if I have new in-laws to enjoy?" she asked Goldie as she offered the big furball some leftover baked chicken, placing it in the white saucer she kept on the porch. "Are you lonely, too, Goldie?"

The cat meowed and lapped up the food, then gave her a long cat stare. Lilah stayed still so he wouldn't run away. But Goldie surprised her by sniffing at her sneakers. She offered her fingers and he sniffed the scent of chicken with a cautious, lingering approach.

"You are a wise cat, always taking your time and doing things slowly and in your own way. I could take a lesson from you."

Goldie stood back, then bounced off the porch and headed toward the gazebo. Lilah followed the cat, laughing at his antics as he jumped and sniffed and tried to use one of the posts to groom his claws.

"Noah wouldn't like that," Lilah told the big tomcat. "He did do a *gut* job on this. So far."

For the most part, the gazebo was nearly finished but he still had to paint it and finish the roof. She wanted to transfer some of the big dish gardens from the front porch to the backyard so she could place them around the pretty structure during the wedding. She and the girls would hang netting and flowers around the octagon-shaped roof.

"I think it's so pretty. Joshua always wanted to build me a pergola or a gazebo. But we ran out of time."

A memory nagged at her brain but she couldn't capture it. Her thoughts moved from the past to the future with a clarity she hadn't seen before.

Did she want to love again? Could she?

"After the wedding," she told Goldie. The cat had curled up on the steps to the gazebo, obviously enjoying his new playhouse. "After this is finished, I'll start thinking toward the future a bit more."

Lilah stepped up into the gazebo and took in the scent of freshly cut wood mixed with a thousand fragrant blossoms.

She silently thanked *Gott* for her garden. And she thanked *Gott* for Noah, too. Sinking down on the top step, she watched as Goldie shot up and ran away.

Alone, Lilah remembered the love that had brought her here and the pain she'd endured after losing Joshua. Her garden had become her refuge and she could see now that she resented Noah interrupting that refuge and changing it. She resented him in the same way Sara resented his presence. They both wanted this little bit of beauty in the yard, but they didn't want the man who'd built it to disrupt their lives.

"You should be here, Joshua. *You*. Not *him*," she said in a shout of pain. "I want you here."

Then she looked up and saw Noah standing

there, staring at her. Before she could say anything, he turned around and stalked back out the side gate.

"Noah," she called. "Noah, come back."

He was gone by the time she made it around the corner.

Noah pulled his bike into the garage at his modest house on the other side of Pinecraft, Lilah's voice still echoing in his head.

"Not him. Not him. Not him."

It shouldn't hurt so much to hear that, and he should have already realized Lilah was still in love with her husband, but hearing her shout it with such conviction and anger had left him defeated and cold, a new kind of grief entering his already broken system. He'd come close to loving again and now the pain of not being able to find that kind of intimacy and happiness with Lilah made him numb with regret. After a few weeks of seeing glimmers of hope and happiness, he felt the full-blown grit of his deep grief returning.

After putting his bicycle away, Noah went inside and watched out the window as the sun began to set , his heart so lonely the physical pain made it hard to breathe.

He'd finish what he'd started. He'd get the gazebo painted and trimmed out in time for the wedding, but after that he'd get his head on straight and pour his heart into his work again. He had houses to build and enough to keep him busy for a lifetime.

A lifetime where he'd still be alone.

How could he go back to the silence of isolation after the wonderful days he'd had with Lilah in her beautiful garden?

Only *Gott* knew the answer to that question.

Lilah couldn't eat or sleep. She poured herself into wedding details, making sure the best of her linens were clean and that the clear plastic plates Ramona had suggested were washed, dried and stacked on the kitchen counter.

The rain started around nine on Monday morning and Noah didn't show up to finish his work. Blaming it on the weather and not what he'd heard her shouting to the world, she tried not to think about how she'd hurt him by flinging her angry words to the wind.

Had her heart spoken what her head couldn't see?

Carol came into the kitchen. "Mamm, you've washed those throwaway plates enough. Isn't this the third time?"

"Maybe," Lilah said, "But I want them to shine."

"Can plastic shine any more than that?" Carol asked, pointing to the clear plates.

"I suppose not." Lilah put down her dish towel. "This rain means the storm is getting closer."

Carol glanced outside. "Sara is worried, but surprisingly she is staying positive."

Lilah wished her daughter had been more accommodating and agreeable early on. But she'd take this news and hope Sara's new attitude prevailed. And she'd need to do the same. "That's something to be joyful about."

Carol studied her, a sweet smile on her face. Her *kapp* was crooked so Lilah reached out to fix it. "Mamm, why are you sad?"

"I'm not sad," Lilah replied. Then she sighed and looked out at the gazebo. "I was hoping Noah could put the finishing touches on that thing and now it's raining."

"Maybe he'll be able to do that later in the week," Carol said, her gaze still on Lilah. "And once Sara is married and all this wedding drama is over, you and Noah will have real time to get to know each other."

"Real time?" Lilah wanted to laugh but her heart refused to go there. "What exactly is real time?"

Carol bobbed her head and leaned in. "Time where you don't feel guilty or like we're all watching you. I like Noah, Mamm. He's nice and he's got a steady income and well, you need to have more fun. I think he could help you with that."

Lilah did laugh then, a giggle spilling over all the worries and regrets in her heart. "You are one smart teenager, Carol. My sweet girl." She gathered Carol in her arms. "A nice, gainfully employed man who can help me have fun. You summed him up."

Then she stopped laughing. "But I think Noah is not too happy with me right now."

Carol didn't ask questions. She just nodded. "Weddings always bring people back together. And I don't see how he could be unhappy with you. You feed him and mostly leave him alone. I hope he shows up at the wedding and makes you smile all day long."

Lilah looked back out at the falling rain and wished it could wash away the words she'd said the other night. Why did she have to rant out loud?

Then she stopped, her head going up. And why had Noah been coming into her yard on a Sunday evening?

The next day, Noah checked on the last row of houses in the far east subdivision near the bay. Another Lantz Seaside community was now ready to be filled with happy tourists and excited locals. The rows and rows of colorful homes with shining tin roofs and sturdy white porch posts were made to withstand everything from hot summers and humid climates to hurricanes and floods. They looked a bit cookie-cutter, but then that's what the public demanded. Like pretty little square cakes, they shone bright and tempting and brought buyers in droves.

He should be happy, but this rain was making him feel morose. Well, that and hearing Lilah's words over and over in his head. Sara wasn't the only one regretting him building their gazebo. He'd give up his houses and any and all gazebos to have his Janeen back. So he understood Lilah's resistance and yet he wished she could move on, that he could move on. That they could find a way to be closer than just friends.

Gott had shown him, however. Lilah wasn't ready and that meant he'd probably be better off alone. He'd gone by there on Sunday to take one last look at the gazebo before he painted it. If he ever got back there, he'd get the painting done and he'd add the fancy finial later. He had to find the right one.

Now he wasn't sure if he could return to Lilah's garden.

But a job was a job. He'd go and do the last of

the work and hope he didn't come face to face with her. Because right now he wasn't sure what he'd do or say.

He had a lot he could say.

Best to let it go for now.

And best to go back to his world where he'd tuck the memories of jasmine and gardenias and roses far back in his dreams, right along with the memories of Lilah's smiles.

Chapter Sixteen

"And we'll make this bedroom a nursery one day," Abram said on Tuesday night while he took his parents and Lilah around the cottage he and Sara would soon share. The girls had moved ahead with Samuel, too impatient to get the full tour. "It's small and perfect for a *kinder*."

"Sooner than later," Sara replied with a glance at Abram. "I can't wait."

Abram indulged her with a quick tug, wrapping an arm over her shoulder. "One step at a time, *liebling*."

Sara's grin deflated a bit. "*Ja*, we will need to get this house finished first, ain't so?"

"That is the first step, after we actually get married," Abram replied, his dark brown eyes glowing with happiness.

Sara laid her head on his shoulder. "Storm or no storm."

Lilah noticed what Carol had pointed out. Sara was in a better mood this last week leading up to the big day. Of course, Sara hadn't seen Noah in the garden in days so that might have something to do with her improved disposition.

"Mamm, are you okay?" Sara asked now, her eyebrows lifted high. "You look upset and you didn't eat much."

Lilah tried to pull on a neutral expression. They had had a lovely dinner of fresh shrimp and lime rice, snap beans and a white chocolate sheet cake for dessert. "Not upset. I'm just thinking of you being here and not at home. I'll need to adjust to that, but I'm very happy for you."

Abram smiled and glanced around. "I can't wait to get this finished and ready for us to start our new life." Then he glanced at Lilah. "I'm expecting a lot of Sunday suppers at your house, too."

"I'd be happy to cook for you," Lilah replied, thinking Abram was a thoughtful person. She wouldn't get all teary-eyed tonight.

Sara patted his arm but held her gaze on Lilah. "A few more days—then we will truly be husband and wife." She added, "But I'll pester you as always, Mamm."

"I'd be disappointed if you didn't," Lilah said, meaning it.

Betty came into the kitchen where some of the gifts had already been opened and put on display. "I'm so glad you two will be close by. And Lilah is right down the street. Perfect."

Almost perfect, Lilah thought as Betty grabbed her arm to show her a lovely flower-embossed pitcher her *aenti* had sent to Sara and Abram.

Lilah could see the love in their eyes as they moved through the house. She remembered that kind of love. She missed the intimacy of having a partner, a soulmate, a helpmate.

By the time the night was over, she had a piercing headache and her heart wasn't far behind. But she thanked Betty for the meal and the fellowship.

"Let Abram drive you home," Betty suggested. "I'll help her finish unpacking, Lilah. You have enough to get done before Saturday."

Tired and near her breaking point, Lilah agreed and soon she sat next to Abram on the front bench and the girls sat behind them.

"Are you really all right with all of this?" Abram asked, glancing over at her. "You sure were quiet tonight."

"Of course I'm all right with you marrying my daughter," she replied. "You are a *gut* man, Abram, and a calming influence on Sara. I couldn't ask for more."

"*Ja*, you could," Carol called from the back. "Mamm is sad because she thinks Noah is angry with her. Sara will be glad to hear that news."

"Carol!" Lilah half turned and shook her head. "I'm fine."

But Abram shot her a worried glance. "What happened between you and Noah?"

"I can't say right now," she whispered, indicating her chin back toward her curious girls. "It was a misunderstanding but I'm afraid our friendship is over because of it."

"What does Sara have to do with this?" he asked in his own whisper. "I know she had concerns after you hired him, but has she interfered with him finishing the gazebo?"

"As much as possible," Dana quipped.

Lilah shot her a warning stare.

"*Neh*, nothing to worry about," Lilah replied. "Not before the wedding anyway. It will all work out, I'm sure. Please, Abram, let this go for now."

Abram didn't ask any more questions, but Lilah knew he was curious. Just one more thing to put on her growing list of concerns. If Abram brought this up to Sara, her daughter would certainly be upset all over again.

While the cart bumped along, she held her shawl close. The rain increased right along with her racing heartbeat, making her think this might be the worst week she'd had since Joshua died.

* * *

Noah went by Tanner's store Wednesday to gather some supplies to finish his work. Tanner had ordered the shiny white paint he needed for the gazebo and it had come in just in time. He'd stalled long enough. Now Noah had no excuses.

After two days of drizzle, the rain had stopped for a while and the tropical storm out in the Gulf seemed to be wobbling toward the west. Maybe it would miss them completely, but he prayed—no matter which way it went—that everyone in its path would be safe.

"Why the grim face?" Tanner asked as he handed Noah two cans of mixed paint. "Aren't you going to see Lilah today?"

"I'm going to paint and finish my work for her, but I doubt I'll see her," Noah replied, shaking his head.

Tanner walked with Noah to his cart behind the store. "Trouble in paradise?"

"Ha, this ain't always paradise around here," Noah said on a sharp hiss.

Tanner scratched his chin. "So you and Lilah are still uncomfortable about your feelings for each other?"

"I was feeling pretty happy about my feelings until I walked up on her talking to…herself…or maybe *Gott*." He glanced out to the busy side street where traffic flowed and people rode by on bikes or carts. The world just kept spinning.

"She doesn't want me there, Tanner. She said she wanted Joshua. That he belonged in her garden. Not me."

"She told you that?"

"She said that as I walked around the corner. Said it with such anger. I heard it loud and clear."

"Does she know you heard?"

"Oh, *ja*. She looked up and saw me but coward that I am, I left."

"Have you tried talking to her since?"

"*Neh*. That was Sunday evening and with all the rain, I haven't had an opportunity to speak with her and there is no need. She doesn't want me around her and hearing her shouting that declaration with such agony in her words has shown me I was wrong to even think we could become close."

Tanner gave him a soft slap on the back. "I think you're *wrong* on that *mei* friend. I think Lilah is struggling to let go because she very much wants you in that garden."

"She seemed firm in her words," Noah replied. "It's hard to forget what I saw and heard."

Tanner nodded. "I understand, but don't give up on her. Finish the work you agreed to do and see how she reacts, Noah. Remember she is going through a lot right now. After the wedding—"

"After the wedding, I won't see her again," Noah replied, his tone quiet and firm. "*Denke*. I'd better get going before the rain comes back."

"Okay." Tanner stared him down. "I'll pray for you and Lilah."

"That I can always use," Noah said, smiling. He left knowing Tanner meant what he'd said. He would pray and that brought Noah some comfort. Because right now he was very *ferhoodled* about *Gott*'s plan for his future. He wished it included Lilah, but he'd just have to pray that wish away.

Lilah was happy to see some sunshine, but nervous because that meant Noah would be back. She hoped, she dreaded, she wished, her pulse jumping each time she heard someone on the street.

What could she say to him?

Sara came into the living room and glanced at her. "Mamm, you're still sitting?"

Lilah glanced up, realizing it was past nine in the morning. "Is there something wrong with sitting for a spell?"

"*Neh*," Sara said as she slid into the chair across from Lilah. "Have you overdone things with the wedding? I know I've been bossy and fidgety and at times, intolerable, but I'm feeling so much better now that the house is coming along and I am finally going to be a bride."

Lilah believed her daughter to be sincere, and yet Sara would never know how much angst her mood swings and pointed comments had hurt others. Especially her own mother.

"I am fine," Lilah said. "Just thinking through these last few days. I hope we haven't forgotten anything."

"Just the gazebo," Sara replied. "Is Noah coming back before the wedding or not?"

"I don't have his agenda, daughter," Lilah retorted before she had time to think.

Sara looked appalled. "Mamm, what's going on?"

"Noah will be here to finish the work, Sara. Stop worrying."

"I'm not worried about that now. I'm concerned about you. You look pale and as if you didn't sleep."

"You can be very observant when you want to."

"Did you two quarrel about the gazebo?" Sara asked, her expression full of shame. "This is all my fault."

Lilah wouldn't go so far as to agree with her, but Sara had a valid point. "This will all be over soon and I can go back to my quiet life."

"Mamm, you like Noah. We all know that. If something has changed that, you need to tell me."

"I don't need to tell anyone anything," Lilah said, relieved that Abram hadn't questioned Sara about this situation. She stood to gather her teacup and saucer, but she stumbled and the cup crashed to the wooden floor and broke in half, spilling the remains of her breakfast tea on the rug.

"I'll clean this up," Sara said, rushing to get a damp towel. "Tea stains are hard to wipe away."

Lilah wanted to laugh. Instead, she burst into tears. "*Ja*, some stains never go away."

Then she ran toward the sanctuary of her bedroom and shut the door. Now she'd gone and done it. Falling apart three days before the wedding would only add more fuel to this fire.

But she couldn't stop the tears she'd held at bay for so long now. Too long. Waves of grief hit her over and over with the same wrath of an angry sea. Her grief merged with her anger and the remnants of what should have been and what might have been.

She'd failed in every way. Now Sara would spin out of control and that, too, would be Lilah's fault. She'd managed to ruin everything is spite of her attempts to do the opposite.

Lilah sank down beside her bed and silently

asked *Gott* to show her the way, to teach her how to find peace again and to keep her family safe and intact throughout the storms of life.

She finally got up and fell across the bed, sleep finally overtaking her. Later waking with a start, she got up, only to find Sara gone and the house quiet. When she looked outside, the sun was shining on a sparkling white Victorian-style gazebo complete with a brass butterfly-shaped finial on top.

Lilah gasped, but she had no more tears to shed. Too late, she saw what had been there all along. *Gott* had sent Noah to her, and she could almost feel Joshua's breath on her neck as she remembered him saying, "One day I hope someone helps you finish your garden, Lilah. *Gott* will provide."

Chapter Seventeen

The next afternoon, with the rain picking up and a moaning wind howling all around him, Noah stayed home to catch up on phone calls regarding hurricane preparation and paperwork to clear in case the storm did hit. Around five, he heard a knock at his door. Wondering who would be out in the heavy rain, he hurried to the front of his long, narrow house and opened the door.

Abram and Sara stood there. Abram gave him a stern nod while Sara held her head down and her hands together over her raincoat.

"May we come in?" Abram asked. "We're on our way to buy some hurricane supplies but we need to speak to you."

"Of course," Noah said, wondering what they could possibly want to talk about. Their house was coming along and the gazebo was finished. They both looked so serious he was afraid the wedding was off. Of course, it would have to be called off if the storm had changed course. He needed to check his weather radio.

He ushered them into the small sitting room. "Would you like some *kaffe*? I just perked a fresh pot."

"I'll take some," Abram said, motioning for Noah to sit down. "I know where the pot is, Noah."

He left in such a hurry, Noah didn't argue. "Sara, do you need something to drink?"

She shook her head and glanced toward the kitchen then sat down. Abram came hurrying back with a white cup full of the strong brew. "I can get you some water."

"*Neh*," she said, finally lifting her head, her gaze on Noah now. "I need to tell you something, Noah. Abram and I had a long talk this morning and I told him how rude and dissatisfied I've been with you while you were building the gazebo."

"It's all right," Noah began, relief washing over him. At least one of the Mehl women had made peace with his presence.

"*Neh*, it is not all right," Sara said, her voice rising. "I've been horrible and mean and resentful, but you see, I had a reason for being so upset."

She wiped her eyes and glanced at Abram.

"Go ahead," he said, putting his cup down. "It's the only way we can get past this."

Worried again, Noah didn't know what to say. "What's going on? Just tell me, please."

Sara took a breath and in that moment, she looked like a young, confused girl. Noah's heart went out to her.

"When my *daed* was so sick," she began, "I used to sit with him. I'd sit and pray that he'd get up and be well. I didn't understand death or what it could do to a family. While I sat, he'd sometimes wake up and mumble things to me, as if he were so worried about this and that, everything. I'd try to calm him and he'd eventually settle back down."

"That must have been awfully sad for you," Noah said, his heart grasping her pain. He'd done much the same sitting with Janeen.

"It was," Sara said. "One day about a week before he passed, he grabbed my hand and whispered, 'Don't say anything to your *mamm* about this, but I never did build that gazebo she talked about. You know, in the backyard?'"

Noah let out a grunt. "Go on."

Tears started falling down Sara's face. "He made me promise that when I was old enough, I'd find someone to build her something special and pretty. A gazebo, if possible."

Abram held her close and nodded. "It's okay."

"I hadn't thought about his words for years, but while I was looking through wedding magazines, I saw a gazebo all decked out in flowers and… I think I had some sort of flashback." She held to Abram's hand. "I remembered Daed saying that to me. He said, 'Find someone who can finish her garden—with a gazebo or a pergola—something pretty. Maybe you can get married there in the garden. Promise me, Sara-bell.'"

She gasped, sobs racking her body. "He always called me Sara-bell. And I heard that over and over in my head when I saw that photo of a gazebo. 'Promise me, Sara-bell.'" She held her shoulders high, then slumped back against her chair. "I had not planned on keeping that promise because I had tried to forget those last horrible days."

Noah suddenly understood. "And when you did remember, you tried to get it done for your wedding and for Lilah, just as you told us that first night."

"*Ja*," she said, gaining her strength back. "But Noah, I never dreamed that promise would bring someone new into my *mamm*'s life. I have been so torn between keeping that promise and trying to keep you and Mamm apart, that I forgot what a special gift my *daed*'s request has provided for me, for Mamm and for you. I'm so very sorry. I wasn't fighting against you. I was fighting against what I thought was right—that Daed wanted someone to build the gazebo, not fall for his wife."

She stood and rushed toward Noah. "I'm so sorry I almost ruined my wedding and my *mamm*'s happiness. I want you to know I won't stand in your way anymore. The gazebo is beautiful, just as I imagined, and I know Daed would agree with me and be so happy that my *mamm* could have a great future with someone who will cherish her the way he did."

Touched and speechless, Noah stood and took her into his arms. "My sweet girl, you have done no wrong. You've been trying to honor your *daed*'s request and I can see how my feelings for your mother would upset you. Sara, you are right—this is a beautiful gift for all of us. Joshua didn't want your mother to be sad. He left her one last gift—the gazebo she always wanted. And you made that happen. You fulfilled your promise."

"*Neh*, he brought her the gift he *really* wanted her to have," Sara said. "Someone to love her. And Noah, she has so much love to give, please don't let my failings keep you from going to her. Will you please come to my wedding and talk to her?"

Shocked and amazed, Noah said, "I'd do that

in a heartbeat, but I don't think your *mamm* wants me there. She isn't over your *daed* yet."

Sara bobbed her head. "She will always love him and so will I, but I'm going to tell her exactly what I've told you. I came close so many times, but I knew this would upset her. Now I think she needs to hear it from me before I get married." Sniffling, she added, "I can't get married knowing my *mamm* is sad and you're still lonely. Neither of you needs to be alone anymore."

She turned to Abram. "We need to find Mamm after we go to the market, so I can explain."

He nodded and gave Noah a grateful smile. "That is the best idea I've heard all week. Then we can truly celebrate our marriage and that gazebo that has caused both joy and sorrow."

Sara stood back and smiled at Noah. "I'm so glad Abram made me tell him what was bothering me. I feel so much lighter now."

Noah hugged her again. "You were carrying a heavy load, young lady. But you are brave and your wisdom has shone through your confusion. I know Lilah will be proud of you and now, this whole venture will be rewarding instead of something she'll regret."

"So you'll be at my wedding then?" She glanced outside. "I mean, if I have a wedding."

"I wouldn't miss it for the world, no matter when you are able to marry this man. And I pray your *mamm* will be glad to see me there."

"Storm or no storm," Abram said. But he gave Noah a concerned glance. "I'm afraid we can't control the weather."

"*Neh*," Noah replied. "But remember that you love each other and that is what matters most in a marriage."

Sara glanced back at him, a soft smile on her face. Her whole expression had softened. Noah could see the peace in her now. The peace he'd prayed for. She had confessed her secret and now she could move on, he hoped. He also hoped if she told Lilah the truth, her *mamm* could see him in a different light now, too.

"Be careful out there and get home soon. I think we'll get more rain and wind later tonight and into tomorrow. Sara, this could all be over by Saturday."

"I certainly hope so," Sara replied.

He walked them to the door, still in shock at what Sara had told him, but now he understood things so much better. After they drove off in Abram's work truck, he stared out into the rain and thanked *Gott* for providing.

Lilah paced the floor, waiting for her girls to get home. The neighbor had just gotten an alert that the storm, which been tracking toward Louisiana to the west, had taken a turn back toward the eastern part of the Gulf and was heading straight for the Florida peninsula at an accelerated pace. There probably wouldn't be a wedding on Saturday due to heavy rain and wind, and if the worst happened, no wedding for a while to come. Sara would be devastated but she'd understand. They had to keep their friends and family safe.

Now, according to the news reports, it might be too late to leave. Traffic was already at a standstill on the bridges as tourists and homeowners were hurrying to leave the bayfront and the barrier islands early so they didn't get trapped. The buses running back and forth from Pinecraft to other areas of the country were canceling trips due to the impending weather. Which meant their relatives from Ohio and Pennsylvania wouldn't be able to make the trip.

Her heart slammed against her chest with a pain that every mother had to have felt. Disappointment, worry, fear and acceptance, all curled together and tangled inside her soul.

Bring them home, she whispered. Her open prayer for safety and nothing more. *Dear* Gott*, take care of all of us.*

Carol and Dana arrived first, their eyes wide, questions spilling over each other. They'd been three doors down with some other girls learning how to make jam from fruit.

"We ran, Mamm," Dana said, her hand lifted toward the park. "A man came and told us the storm had changed direction,"

"I'm scared," Carol added. "We heard the roads are crowded and no buses are coming to help us."

Lilah nodded and tugged them close. "We will find a way to get to the big shelter if possible." Then she gave them a reassuring look. "If we can't get out, we'll go to the storage closet between the kitchen and living room. The big one Daed built."

"Daed always knew what to do," Carol said. "You told us that and I do remember little bits and pieces."

"Hold onto those bits and pieces," Lilah said. "They are precious."

"Where's Sara?" Dana asked, glancing around the room. "The storm might get close during the night. What about the wedding?"

Lilah held up her hand and stood to study the rain. "First things first. Your sister is with Abram and so we know she'll be safe if they can't make it home. As for the wedding, we can't have it with a hurricane on the way. It will be disappointing, but Ramona, Martha and I have a Plan B. So don't fret about that. Your sister will be married, but probably not on Saturday. We will see what happens tomorrow. And finally, no matter what happens, we will be fine. *Gott* will provide. Understand?"

They both nodded. Then Dana said, "I want Sara home, Mamm."

"I want that, too," Lilah added as the sky grew dark. Ramona called, telling her she'd managed to move most of the food she'd prepared ahead of time into Tanner's big freezer at the store. "He has a generator there, so the food won't go to waste." Then her friend had said, "The rest is in *Gott*'s hands."

Lilah thanked her friend, then glanced out the front window.

The storm had been tossing rain and spinning outer rain bands all week as it wobbled near the Keys and then shifted toward Louisiana and Texas. Now it was twisting back around, but no one could predict exactly where it would hit. Near Sarasota or St Petersburg, she'd heard from the neighbor.

She stood there with the girls, watching and waiting. Finally, she said, "Let's prepare. We need candles and flashlights. I have water jugs I've stored up all summer. We can use that to cook if we need to, and we'll bathe with it and use the big wipes I bought back in the winter. We have crackers and store-bought soup and the soup I canned during the winter. We can make peanut butter and jelly sandwiches with some of the bread I've frozen. We have enough daylight to pull the hurricane shutters and wooden boards over the windows if we hurry."

Carol and Dana both gave her long, scared gazes. Then they went to work, scattering like little lambs to get the supplies they might need. Lilah went to the storage closet and began moving things to trunks and other rooms and closets. This closet was tucked in the middle of the house underneath the sturdy stairs to a small attic. She rarely went up there, but the extra layer of protection would make her feel better about being cloistered with her girls in the roomy closet with the slanted ceiling, surrounded on all sides by walls. Joshua had built it into the house when they were renovating for just such a purpose. They'd used it a couple of times during storms, but never a full-blown hurricane. Would it suffice?

An hour later, they'd managed with the help of neighbors to get most of the small windows covered with plywood. Then she and the neighbor's husband tugged together the heavy tin shutters over the big front windows.

After thanking her neighbors for their help, Lilah wondered where Sara and Abram were. She had the burner phone for emergencies and she'd tried to call Abram's work phone, but no answer. Knowing he'd do anything to protect her daughter, Lilah focused on what she should take care of next. Most of the Amish homes here had either been updated to hurricane standards or built new to meet the standards, so they were fairly sturdy. Joshua had updated their home before he'd passed, out of his concern for his family. She'd had Nathan and several other men check it each year so she hoped it would survive.

Earlier as they'd hurried to put the shutters on, she'd stood outside in her rain poncho by the kitchen window and her heart had lurched when she'd glanced at the white gazebo sparkling through the dark sky. The constant wind seemed to be growing stronger. The drizzle of rain continued, making the colorful garden look eerie as nighttime approached.

All of her beautiful blossoms would be crushed or blown away. But none of that mattered now.

She had her children to think about.

And she had Noah on her mind and in her heart. She sure wished he could be here now. But she'd managed with one outburst to send him away forever.

Too late, she thought. *I didn't see what I*

needed to see. And now he'll never return to my garden.

Then she realized she hadn't even paid Noah for his work. She'd remedy that, at least, once this storm had passed.

Chapter Eighteen

Noah paced from the front of his house to the back, his updated storm tarps in place and his supplies all safe in a big canvas duffle bag. The storm had advanced and strengthened in the last few hours.

He thought of Lilah and the girls across town from him. Every cell in his body wanted to go there and be with them, but he couldn't intrude where he wasn't wanted. Sara's explanation covered her reasons for resenting his presence, but nothing but grief and love could explain Lilah's words as she sat on the gazebo steps, agony coloring her pretty face.

The gazebo he'd built for her. Him, not Joshua. He wished Joshua could have finished her garden but that hadn't happened. What was so wrong with Noah doing the work, with Noah wanting to get closer to Lilah and her girls?

He paced again, the wind and rain howling against the sturdy vinyl tarp-like material covering the few windows in his long narrow little home. Janeen had loved this house and her touch was still everywhere.

Now even this small two-bedroom cottage seemed too big and lonely for him. Should he just get in his big truck and go see if Lilah was okay?

He'd about decided to do that when he heard a fast knock.

Noah rushed toward the thick wooden door and carefully opened it a few inches, bracing against the wind and rain. "Who is it?"

"It's Abram. I have Sara with me. We need your help."

Noah opened the door wide. Abram was carrying Sara. She moaned and said, "Put me down. I told you I'm all right."

Abram glanced around but held her tight. "In a minute."

"What happened?" Noah asked as he ushered them in. He motioned toward the sofa. "Put her there."

"We got caught in heavy rain and wind," Abram explained as he gently laid Sara down. "We stopped to help someone."

Noah grabbed a blanket and Abram wrapped it around Sara. She moaned and opened her eyes. "I'm okay."

"Just rest for now," Abram told her. Then he

turned to Noah. “We were trying to get back home after going to the big box store—it was packed and most everything was gone already so it took forever. We got back into traffic and were almost past your street when we came up on a tree that had blocked one of the main roads. I got out to help an older couple. They were on foot and had a lot of groceries, but the tree was blocking their way home.”

Noah listened as he heated water for tea. “And?”

Sara moaned again and lifted her head. “And when Abram tried to pull back on the road, the truck got stuck in the mud and the rain kept coming and I tripped trying to help Edna—that was the older woman—and skinned both my legs. But I’m okay. It just hurts to walk.”

“Don’t move,” he told Sara. “I’ll be right back.”

Noah found bandages and more towels, along with a first aid kit. Abram handed Sara a towel, then wiped his face and hair.

Outside, the wind howled and hissed while the rain charged along the already flooded street like a raging river pouring over a dam.

Putting his damp towel on the kitchen table, Abram said, “My truck is still up on the main road right past the turnoff to your street, stuck on the grassy median. I didn’t realize how soggy that spot of grass had become, but it's full of water. The more the tires spun, the more embedded my truck became. We tried to call for help but the lines are so busy we couldn't get through."

"We finally walked with Edna and Ted, guiding them as best we could," Sara said. "They live two streets over from you and offered us shelter."

"But we decided to come here once we knew they were safe," Abram told Noah. "You're alone, and you're family. Plus, you can help us get in touch with people."

Noah's breath caught against his throat. *Family*. He had not heard words like that in a long time. "You'll be safe here. This is one tough little house."

"I'm worried about my *mamm*," Sara said. "We were hoping you'd take us to her. And we have to let Abram's parents know we're okay."

Again, Noah was surprised. "You'd be safer staying here," he said. "You're wet and hurt. I can call Abram's *daed* and he can get word to your *mamm*."

"So you don't want to call her or see her?" Sara asked, fear in every word. "Even though she's all alone, too, with my sisters. They must be so scared."

"I want to see her more than I want to breathe,"

Noah admitted, "but I also don't want to upset her."

Sara sat up, her fingers grasping the warm teacup Noah offered her. "If you get her and my sisters here safely, or even if you make it to their house and stay with them, I'll tell her everything, Noah. I will make it right between you two."

Noah glanced at Abram. "Use my landline to call your folks. Then call Lilah and warn her I'm coming. Surely she won't turn me away in a storm."

"But will it be safe for you to drive in this?" Abram asked. "I'd go with you but I can't leave Sara."

"I'll be fine," Noah said. "I have that big truck that can withstand just about anything. You two have been through enough. Call your folks and I will do my best to either bring Sara's family here, or I'll stay there with them."

He touched a hand to Sara's arm. "Get your skinned knees doctored and bandaged. You don't want Lilah to see your injuries just yet."

Sara nodded. "Noah, I know you'll keep her safe. *Denke*."

Noah grabbed a light raincoat and a canvas hat, then found his truck keys and the powerful flashlight he kept in the entryway cabinet. He'd get to Lilah even if he had to swim.

* * *

Lilah and the girls stayed close to the open closet, ready to hurl themselves inside if the wind picked up more. It howled and groaned, shaking the shuttered house. They still had power but she expected that to end soon. The very earth seemed to shake and bounce each time a heavy gust hit the house. Not being able to see out was almost as bad as hearing that wind crashing against the earth.

Just like she'd not seen what Sara and Noah had figured out—she needed that gazebo to help her heal, and she needed Noah in her life to help her trust and love again. No wonder Sara had fought against him being there. Her daughter recognized the attraction and awareness between them right away. And her dear Joshua had foreseen and blessed this—he'd wanted someone to help her finish her garden.

She needed to tell both Noah and Sara that she understood now and that she appreciated what they'd done for her. She'd thought she should avoid Noah because of Sara. But she should have gone with her instincts. Instead she'd lashed out and said something she regretted. She would always love Joshua but now things had changed. So much.

Where was Sara? She'd prayed silently while trying to keep Carol and Dana calm. Abram had not answered his phone and she didn't know if his parents had a phone at all. He should have brought Sara home by now. They were only running last-minute errands.

"I hope Sara is safe," Dana said again. "I can't read this devotional anymore, Mamm. I'm too worried."

"You don't have to read," Lilah told her, taking the small book and tucking it away. "We can just talk."

Carol scooted closer to Lilah. "Like when we were *kinder* and you'd talk to us before we went to sleep. I loved those times."

Lilah kissed her daughter's head. "I've neglected you two but once this wedding is done, we are going to take a day and go down to the beach. We'll have a picnic and chase each other in the surf, ain't so?"

"Oh, I'd love that," Dana said. "Do you think the water will come this far inland during the night?"

Lilah listened to the wind, her heartbeats jumpy and jittery. "I don't think so but I can't be sure. We know *Gott* will provide. And he gave us the *gut* sense to be prepared since it's too late to get out of here."

"I hope He will provide a boat," Carol said with a slight grin. "I mean, I'm praying."

"*Ja*, let's pray," Lilah told her daughters as

she held them both on each side of her there against the wall, the house shaking and creaking around them. When they heard a crash and then a boom, Lilah pulled the girls inside the big closet. "Our power just went out, but we have candles and our flashlights. And we're together."

"But we don't know where Sara is," Carol replied, her voice cracking. "What if something happens to her?"

Dana started crying. "Sara might miss her own wedding."

"Shh." Lilah held them, her fears mounting, her prayers pushing back on those fears. "She is with Abram. He will keep her safe."

She prayed.

Noah's big truck shuddered each time a wind gust hit it. He held the steering wheel with a white-knuckle grip while he drove through the washed-out roads at a pace that allowed him to see only a few feet in front of the vehicle. All around, cars were stalled and trees were down. And the storm hadn't hit land yet.

What should have been minutes seemed to be taking hours. He could walk it better, but he didn't want to leave his truck abandoned. He'd surely need it once the storm had passed.

He came up on the turn right toward Lilah's

house when the wind picked up and blasted against the vehicle. Then Noah heard a crash and looked up to see a huge oak limb heading for his windshield. He ducked just as it hit, the windshield groaning and shattering like a glass pitcher being hit by a baseball bat.

Then everything went black.

Lilah woke with a start, her phone buzzing in her pocket.

The girls stirred from their blankets and sat up, waiting for her to find her emergency phone.

"Sara?" she asked, not knowing who it could be.

"Lilah, it's Betty Troyer. Abram called us and he and Sara are safe."

"Oh, what a relief," Lilah said, tears burning hot against her eyes. She nodded to the girls. "Where are they?"

Betty cut in and out, static hissing through the phone. "Betty?"

"Noah's place," Lilah heard, disbelief curling in her stomach.

"Did you say they're at Noah's?"

"*Ja*, it's a long story but they had to go back there. Trees down everywhere. I'll keep you posted."

"*Denke*," Lilah said, confused and even more worried. "Did you talk to Noah?"

"*Neh*," Betty said, the static getting worse. "He left. He was on his way to—"

The call was dropped. Lilah asked in a loud voice, "On his way to where, Betty?"

She tried calling back but it kept ringing and ringing.

"Mamm, what happened?" Carol asked, grabbing Lilah's wrist. She took the phone away. "Mamm?"

"Sara and Abram are safe at Noah's house. Betty said Noah was on his way somewhere, but the call ended before Betty could tell me where."

"Why were they at Noah's house?" Dana asked. "That makes no sense."

"*Neh*, it doesn't," Lilah replied. "They are safe and for now, I'll take that. I'm sure there's an explanation. They must have gotten caught in the storm and his was the closest place to find shelter."

But Betty said they'd gone *back* to Noah's house. What had they been doing there with a storm coming?

And where had Noah been going, all alone in the worst part of the storm?

"What should we do?" Carol glanced from Lilah to Dana, the faint glow of the battery-powered lantern standing in the corner showing her wide eyes and taut expression.

Lilah wasn't sure how to answer that. She wanted to run out into the storm and find Noah, and she also wanted her other daughter here with them so she could hold her close.

Gathering her thoughts, she refused to scare her girls.

"We stay here where we are safe," Lilah replied. "And we pray that Noah is safe out there. He must have gotten an urgent call from someone."

Someone he really cared about if he was willing to risk his life out in this weather.

Noah's head hammered a pain that felt like rocks hitting his brain. The tree limb had just grazed his temple, but the smaller limb jutting from it had knocked against his head. Now his shattered windshield lay in shards all over the truck seats and his clothes. Brutal wind and chilling rain hit against the cuts and lacerations on his face and arms.

But he was alive and he needed to get out of this truck. Only the door wouldn't open because part of the tree was wedged against it. He'd have to climb over to the other side, but that meant avoiding jagged shards of broken glass and more stabbing tree twigs and small limbs. One big limb had wreaked havoc with his sturdy vehicle.

But that was nothing compared to him wanting to get to Lilah's house. So he managed to get his seat belt off, and with bloody hands and an old towel he kept to wipe the windows when the humidity was high, he shoved at the glistening broken glass and managed to maneuver his body across the console and onto the other seat without getting any more cuts. Once he'd caught his breath and the dizziness subsided, he worked on getting that door open. Nothing was blocking it so after a few tries with burning wounds, he let out a grunt and shoved it open.

Rain and wind hit him, stinging his injuries and blinding his eyes, but Noah stood and made sure he was on the right street. His lightweight raincoat was shredded from the glass. Thankfully, his flashlight and his pocket radio were both intact. He could find his way if he didn't pass out, and then he'd dry the radio and find out exactly where the storm was headed.

Steadying himself, he held onto the truck and then pushed off, taking a couple of small steps. He had to stop and grab onto a palm tree as a gust of wind threatened to push his wobbly legs out from under him, but he kept at it. He couldn't run, but he stayed on the flooded sidewalk and watched for any help.

The roads were quiet, a few abandoned vehicles sitting awkwardly here and there as the water began to rise. Those cars would be pushed around even more when this thing reached land.

It had been raining solid now for about ten hours and the tide would determine how far this water would push inward.

He stopped when he saw a bench and took a moment to sit and catch his breath, the storm making him shiver and hold his arms against his aching body.

"Maybe this wasn't the best idea," he shouted to the wind.

All around him, houses were boarded up with hurricane shutters, tarps, and plywood. He had no idea if the true storm was advancing toward Sarasota and Pinecraft, but it had sent out enough rainbands to bring down trees. That and being located on the eastern side of the storm's spin was enough to convince him there was more to come.

Which is why he didn't mind being out here or being injured so much. He had to get to Lilah before the worst of this thing hit. He had to make her see that they belonged together.

If they could get through this night, they might be able to make it together for the rest of their lives.

Determined and rested, Noah stood, the wind pushing at his wet clothes and his freezing body. He had to take a breath and fight nature with every step, the gusts trying to topple him as he bent over and splashed through the dirty, cold water now flowing all around him. Watching each step for debris and broken tree limbs, he jumped back as a long snake moved like floating rope two feet away from him.

"Keep on moving, fellow," Noah said, his words lost on the wind. "And I'll do the same."

Then he glanced up and saw Lilah's house just a few feet away, there on the corner. Noah found his strength and tugged himself forward while the wind fought him like a warrior out for revenge.

He finally made it up the steps, crawling and clawing, rain running off the roof to drench him. Grabbing the doorknob, he shifted and tried to stand but everything started spinning and his legs started to give out, causing him to stumble and fall onto the porch floor.

Noah banged on the door with his flashlight, every inch of his body hurting now. He kept banging until the darkness took over again and the flashlight slipped out of his hand and went rolling away on the wet porch. Then he passed out.

Chapter Nineteen

"I heard knocking," Carol said, lifting off the old blankets with all the fury of a kite taking to the wind. "Someone is here. Maybe it's Sara."

Lilah and Dana managed to uncurl and get up, too. "Wait, don't open that door until I get there," Lilah shouted to Carol.

They all rushed toward the door, a solid heavy piece that was now fighting a determined, raging wind.

"Who is it?" Lilah called out. "Sara?"

No answer. She couldn't see through the window shutters so Lilah had no choice but to open the door, which they hadn't shuttered. "I can't leave whoever it is out there."

"But the wind, Mamm," Carol warned. "It could sweep us away."

"Stand back," she said, shooing the girls out of the way. "The wind will hurl through here and you could get knocked down, so hold onto something. I'll get the door open and you two help whoever is out there to get inside. We could have heard a branch flying onto the porch."

The girls both nodded and gave each other reassuring glances.

"Ready?"

"Ready," Carol said. Dana didn't look so sure.

Lilah unlocked the door and used all her strength to hold it steady, but when she opened it, she screamed. Noah was passed out on the wet porch, soaked and unconscious, and covered with cuts and bruises.

"Noah," Carol screamed, dragging him by one arm, Dana helping with the other arm. "Mamm, he's stuck."

Lilah held the door, but Noah was now blocking it. She couldn't get it shut. Rain pushed by the wind and drenched all of them within minutes.

Carol tried again to get Noah inside. "Mamm, I can't."

Lilah let go of the door, the wind forcing it out of her hands with a bang. With all her strength, she gathered Noah's legs and pushed while the girls pulled.

"He's in," Carol called out. "Shut the door."

Lilah whirled and tried but the force of the storm held the door back. It would snap soon if she didn't do something. With a grunt and a deep breath, she strained against the heavy wood. The girls ran to help, pushing and shoving until they managed to push the door partway against the hurricane strength of the wind.

"It's like pushing a rock uphill," Carol called, her face soaking wet.

"One more time," Lilah, equally soaked, shouted. "All together."

She and the girls pushed and grunted and fought until finally the door won over the roaring wind. It slammed back closed with a bang but Lilah held it with her back against it until she could lock it tight, praying the hinges wouldn't give way.

Then she fell back against the door, the girls beside her.

They looked at each other, then looked at Noah, lying there soaking wet and hurt.

"Now we know where he was headed," Dana said. "He was trying to get to you, Mamm."

"Get me towels and water and bring the rubbing alcohol and bandages." Lilah got a pillow and put it underneath Noah's head, then checked his pulse. "He's alive, but something happened. He's hurt."

"If he tried to get here in a cart, that probably didn't work," Dana said in a pragmatic tone. "Maybe he walked."

"His house is a good way from ours," Lilah said. "He does have that big work truck."

"Maybe it's parked somewhere and he ran here?"

They speculated while they moved him out of the hallway and rolled him onto a dry blanket. Then Lilah saw the large lump on his right temple. "He's been hit."

She leaned over him, cleaning each wound, worried that the storm waters could be contaminated. "Noah, can you hear me? It's Lilah. What happened?"

"He's not waking," Dana said. "Are you sure he's breathing?"

"He's breathing," Carol told her. "His chest is lifting up."

"Noah?" Lilah's heart hurt, thinking of him out in this hurricane. "Why are you here?"

He moaned and tried to move. But when he winced and went still, Lilah knew his injuries were worse than just surface cuts. "I think he has a concussion," she said. "And possibly hurt ribs or worse, something internal going on."

"What should we do?" Carol asked. "We can make tea if the propane tank is okay."

"We have no way of knowing if the tank is still there," Lilah replied. "But we have room temperature water. We can steep some strong tea in that, at least."

"I'll get it started," Dana told them, moving with a flashlight toward the kitchen. "We can heat it over the lantern, can't we?"

"Good idea," Carol said. "But it will take some time."

"We've got all night," Lilah said. "But I need to wake him up. I've heard it's not good to sleep too much with a concussion."

The girls scurried away while she found more pillows and covered Noah with another dry blanket. They'd managed to get him out of the shredded raincoat but the rest of his wet clothes had soaked the other blankets and towels.

"Noah," she said, tears burning in her tired eyes, "Noah, please wake up and tell me why you did such a reckless thing?"

She turned to get more alcohol when a firm hand gripped her arm. "I wanted to check on you," he said, lifting his head. "Why else would I be so foolish?"

Then he closed his eyes and went back to sleep.

Only Lilah wouldn't let him sleep. He was so weary and he hadn't slept well in days. Why couldn't he just stay in that dark, unknowing dream?

"Noah, you need some tea and medication," he heard her telling him again, her voice whispering at times and loud at other times. Mad at him again, was she?

"Noah, please," he heard now against the constant moaning wind. "I have so much to tell you. I'm so sorry."

He tried to think but his mind roiled and coiled like live electrical wire. Something important? He needed to tell her something. But what?

He only wanted to sleep. He drifted back into the darkness only to be roused again.

"Noah, you have a concussion and you're injured. We can't get help right now, but if you wake up I can find out where you hurt."

He tried to lift his hand to his heart, but that was too much effort. "Here, Lilah," he said in his head. But she didn't respond. "Here, Lilah."

He slept, dreaming of beautiful, ethereal gardens and a lovely woman walking toward him. Janeen? *Neh.* Someone else.

In what seemed like seconds, he became fully awake and his whole body screamed with pain.

"Lilah?"

"I'm here," she said from the left.

She was sitting against the wall, a big pillow behind her.

"Where are we?" he asked as she scooted over to hold a wet rag to his head.

"You're in my house on the floor by the storage closet."

"Don't recall getting invited in."

"The storm got you, but you made it here and passed out. We had to drag you inside."

"Carol? Dana? Are you all okay?" he asked, glancing around while his head did a tap dance of a protest. "How did I get here?"

"We don't know," Lilah replied. "Can you sit up? You don't need to sleep with that concussion."

He lifted and winced. "I think I must have cracked a rib."

"Then stay." She placed several pillow behind his back and head. "We think you came out in the storm to check on us. Do you remember how you got here? Your cart or your truck?"

"Truck," he said. "Truck."

"Here, sip this," she said. "It's weak tea, but the little bit of caffeine can help you."

He drank the tea, thinking it tasted like nectar. "*Denke*."

"So do you remember anything?" she asked.

Noah studied her, noticing her head was bare and her hair coiled in a long gold-colored braid against her dress. He shouldn't stare but she was sure a beautiful sight after the night he'd had.

"I am remembering now," he admitted. "I

took the truck to come and check—Sara wanted me too—demanded it, really."

Lilah smiled at that, then frowned right behind the smile. "Why were she and Abram at your house, Noah?"

Noah's memories floated by, washed up with the storm waters, murky and dark, deep, too deep to reach just yet. "I can't remember."

Lilah dozed, Noah on one side of her and the girls curled up together in the open closet right by her other side. She'd stayed here with Noah in case they had to help him into the safe room they'd set up earlier. The storm had hovered over them, full of fury and rage, battering the creaking house.

When she awoke, the light behind the shutters had begun to change and the wind had died down, making her think daylight was coming. She had no idea what time it was—no power yet and she hoped the propane tank was still there. And no word from Sara and Abram. Normally, she would have been appalled that they'd been left in a house together with no one to chaperone, but storms changed proprieties. Now she was thankful Sara had made it to Noah's home, for whatever reason, and that Abram had been with her. She prayed the house had held up.

But the nagging question lingered, and right

now, Noah couldn't answer it. Why had her daughter, who'd been so against Noah, gone back to his house to demand he come to check on Lilah?

Shaking her head, she stumbled up and then realized something. The house wasn't shaking and the rain sounded like only a drizzle.

They'd made it through the storm.

Relief washed over her, followed by regret. The yard had to be a big mess. She let out a gasp.

What about the gazebo? Careful not to wake the girls and worried that she'd fallen asleep instead of trying to keep Noah awake, she scooted away and grabbed onto a chair to stand. She prayed he'd be okay and that this sleep was needed to help him mend.

Then she went to the back door, glad it was heavy wood and just as sturdy as the big front door. Did she dare open it? Grabbing a shawl, she wrapped it against her dress and took a deep breath. She had to see what might be left of the garden she'd worked on for so long.

Then she braced herself, knowing it would be a mess after all that torrential wind and rain. She didn't expect to see anything left.

She'd just stepped out onto the porch, her hands going to her mouth, when she heard someone behind her.

"Lilah?"

Noah stood there, crooked and clearly in pain. She blinked back tears and reached for him. "*Kumm* and see."

He came to her and took her hand. "We'll be okay, Lilah. You hear? We'll be okay."

Together, they took it all in while they held on to each other, the light remnants of rain left from last night's hurricane dripping with precise softness all around the porch while silent tears fell down Lilah's face.

"The gazebo, Noah." She pointed toward the white structure. "It's still there."

Noah clutched the damp porch post, pain radiating all over his body. The gazebo was intact, but the finial was missing. But he didn't know if Lilah had even noticed it since it had rained so much after he'd placed it on top of the domed roof.

"My yard," she said, tears glistening on her cheeks. "It's all gone."

The yard looked like someone had turned it upside down and dumped all the pretty flowers onto the ground. Palm fronds lay scattered here and there. Jasmine blossoms covered the wet green grasses with little white-and-yellow blossoms, rose petals lay scattered along the paths and hibiscus leaves floated on puddles of water.

"It's like a messy quilt," she said, putting a hand on his arm. "But we got through it, ain't so."

"*Ja*," Noah said. "Lilah, it looks like a beautiful portrait, too. A portrait that proves *Gott*'s beauty is always something to marvel about."

She lifted her head and glanced around. "Every bloom stripped and tossed and yet some of them are still vivid and undamaged. How did they survive that wind?"

"Their lightness, I reckon," he replied, wishing he could wipe her tears away. "They must have floated down and let the water take them."

"Until the water drained away and left us a few."

Noah moved closer and put his hand across her back. "We made it through and so did some of those blossoms."

Lilah chuckled. "You always see the bright side, and I try, but I can definitely see it today."

Noah tugged her close. "I could have died last night. Everything is bright from here on out."

Then she slapped his arm. "Why did you take such a risk, Noah? Why would Sara even be at your house?"

"That's a long story," he said. Then he leaned on the railing.

"Oh, I'm sorry," Lilah said, her hand still on his arm. "Let's get you inside. The propane tank seems to be okay so that means fresh coffee and a hot breakfast."

"I'd like that. And while you're at it, if you have any heavy gauze or material, we need to wrap my ribcage. I'm pretty sure one of my ribs is cracked."

"Of course," she said, helping him back toward the kitchen. "The garden can wait for now. But I don't think we'll be having a wedding here tomorrow."

"You're wrong," came a voice from inside the house.

Lilah looked to see Sara standing there with Abram. He and Lilah had not heard them come in.

"Oh, oh, you're all right," she said, still holding to Noah. "Abram, will you help him to the sofa. He got injured last night and we haven't even found out what happened."

"We know what happened," Abram said, taking Noah and walking him across to the living room. "We saw your truck up on the main road. Looks like you turned onto this street just as a giant limb came loose from a tall pine. Your truck is covered in pine branches and your windshield is shattered."

Noah nodded. "*Ja*, that's it. That's what happened." He touched his face, only now realizing some of his cuts had bandages on them. Then it all came pouring back, his memories too fresh to process. “I got hit in the head and couldn’t get my bearings for a while there.”

Lilah ran to Sara and hugged her. The girls were awake and they both jumped up to see Sara. Then they prattled on about their night while Lilah kept staring at Sara. She finally glanced back at Noah. “*Denke* for giving them shelter. You should have stayed there with them.”

Noah couldn’t answer the questions she’d asked earlier. That would be up to Sara. She needed to let her *mamm* know why she’d been so hesitant about him building the gazebo.

Abram caught Noah up on things. “Your house is still there. It was a rough night. We got in the hallway with candles and flashlights, plenty of pillows to protect us. You have some trees down and the power is out. Might be missing a few shingles.”

“I’m glad to hear that.” Noah gave Sara a quick glance, “Your *mamm* was terribly worried and I couldn’t explain anything in my condition.”

“He’s right. I need some explanations.” Lilah waited for everyone to finish talking, then asked Sara, “But first, why am I wrong? You don’t plan to go ahead with the wedding, do you?”

Chapter Twenty

Lilah knew a speaking look when she saw one. Sara and Noah were up to something and she was afraid to know what it was. But they seemed on better terms so maybe it had something to do with the wedding.

"Sara, what is the plan?" she asked again, the sight of her damaged garden foremost in her mind. "You haven't even been out back."

Sara smiled at Abram. After he'd checked Noah over, he came and stood by her. "We had a long time to talk last night," he said. "This was a bad storm—at least a Category Two hurricane from what we've heard from people we talked to while coming here. But for us, it was a blessing of sorts."

Sara leaned her head on Abram's shoulder. "*Ja*, for once it was just us and neither of us had to rush away. We couldn't rush away. So we held close and just opened our hearts to be honest about everything."

Abram's smile beamed. "We had a lot to get through, but we are so happy this morning. And we decided because we love each other, nothing else matters. We could have been hurt last night when my truck got bogged down. But instead, we helped an older couple get home and that led us back to Noah's house."

"But you had Noah come over here," Lilah interrupted. "Do you want to explain that?"

Sara nodded at Noah. "I can explain—"

"—I wanted to come, Lilah," he said, interrupting Sara. "I was about to leave to come here when they showed up, wet and tired. I gave them shelter, but Sara was worried about you. She did demand that I come, but I didn't need to be persuaded. My heart was already telling me I needed to be here with you and the girls."

Lilah let out a sigh. "Soon, someone is going to tell me what's really going on. But for now, I'm glad we are all safe and the storm is over." Then she smiled. "What is your plan for the wedding, daughter?"

"Well, I didn't get to finish," Sara replied. "Abram and I want to be married tomorrow in your backyard and we don't care if there are no blossoms or guests or food or cake. We only want to be married. Our new house has some damage, but we will fix that right up. Tomorrow is our wedding day and no storm is going to stop that."

Then she whirled past all of them like a dust cloud. Staring out at the yard, she gasped. "*Ja*, the yard is ruined but, Mamm, your gazebo is still there."

Lilah glanced at Noah. "Yes, but the butterfly is missing."

He smiled at her. "It's missing its top but we might find that somewhere in all this rubble."

"That butterfly was a nice gesture, Noah." She hadn't found a time to tell him about her revelation after she'd seen the complete project. When would there be a *gut* time for that?

Carol and Dana stood with Sara, the three of them silent and still as they took in the damage.

"We still have flowers," Dana said. "They are everywhere. We can put them in water for the wedding."

"*Gut* idea," Sara said, smiling at her groom and then at Noah. "We'll need to check with Ramona on the food, but Tanner's generator should have helped with that." She tickled Dana's ribs and pushed at Carol's hair. "We'll make do, like Mamm always says."

Lilah's shock at this new attitude showed on her face. "I do always say that."

Sara looked at Lilah. "And Mamm, I'll explain everything about being at Noah's. I hope you'll forgive me when I do."

Lilah shook her head. "After all of this, I think I can forgive just about anything. A wedding it is! Tomorrow."

Then she started calling out orders. "Abram, I need you to find that roll of gauze we had for Carol's injured ankle, and then you and I will wrap Noah's rib. Girls, gather in the kitchen and make toast. We'll have grits and eggs with it. And bring out the good jam—that wild cherry I save for Christmas."

"We are truly celebrating," Carol said to Dana.

"We are, but before we get carried away about the wedding," Lilah said, "we need to get out and see the damage. I'm sure there are others who might need our help."

"*Gut* plan," Abram replied. "My folks are okay, but the whole community has a lot of downed trees and some flooding in the park near the creek. You just missed that in your yard, Lilah."

"We heard it was a Two that almost became a Three before it hit land just north of here," Sara said. "I'll never forget this night."

"Me, either," Noah said from the couch.

The chatter started back up as they all had hurricane tales to tell.

Despite his pain, Noah couldn't stop smiling. He hadn't been this content in a long time. He'd finally found a family for himself if they'd have him.

When Lilah and Abram came to nurse him, she said, "Let's get him into the washroom and take his shirt off. The girls don't need to see this."

She blushed as she said it, but Abram only laughed. "I'll be the chaperone this time, Lilah."

"I don't know what you mean," she said, teasing Abram.

She blushed even more, but as they helped Noah up, she gave him an encouraging smile. And he hoped he knew what she meant by that smile.

The next few hours were a blur for Lilah. They got Noah's hurt rib wrapped after Abram had put some ointment on to soothe the area. She gave Noah some pain pills and made him promise to see the first doctor they could find. He'd insisted on going out with them, telling her he'd been through worse at construction sites. Lilah had finally given in.

The girls put on their rain shoes and they started to walk through the neighborhood, checking on people and explaining to those invited to the wedding that it would still happen tomorrow. The rain had tapered off and the weather radios were predicting sunshine later in the day, but tree limbs, branches, and debris had landed all along the route, making it hard to get around. The storm had moved on up through Florida and Georgia. It had caused several tornados along the state line where Florida, Alabama, and Georgia all met. Now it was breaking apart somewhere in Tennessee.

But here in Pinecraft, *Englisch*, Mennonites and Amish were out and about, helping to move limbs and branches or pick up trash and pile it on the side of the road. Some houses looked worse than others, but no one had been killed.

One neighbor offered his golf cart so Abram could drive Noah. Lilah could see the pain etched on Noah's handsome face, so she was thankful he didn't argue.

They were on their way into town when they met up with Tanner and Martha. Eva remained home with the children.

"I stayed with them last night," Martha explained. "What a storm. Ramona's place is a mess, so she's going to come to my house for a while—just until she can get things repaired. But all the food we cooked for the wedding is still in Tanner's big freezer with the generator keeping it cold. What's the plan for the wedding?"

Lilah waited for Sara to speak up.

Which she did, immediately. "We are getting married in the garden tomorrow. The water has receded as fast as it came through, but the yard might be a bit mushy."

"Well, so will I," Martha replied, wiping her eyes. "That's the most romantic thing I've ever heard."

Abram let out a laugh. "*Ja*, because getting married in the mud can only put us on solid ground later, right?"

"Exactly," Martha said. "It just means you two truly get what being married is all about." Then she went right back to business. "Lilah, I'll let Ramona know the wedding is on. We'll need to heat up the food and we can do that in shifts between my oven and yours."

After they'd formed a plan, Martha hurried off to find Ramona. Then they came to the café where Sara worked.

"Look, Mamm," Sara said. "Albert has the café open. I guess he has a generator, too. Let's get something to eat."

They went into the crowded little café and Albert waved to Sara. "I know you're supposed to be getting married, but I could use some help here."

Sara glanced at Abram. "Would you mind?"

"*Neh*," he said. "I'd like to help out myself."

Alicia came out of the kitchen. "Sara, you're okay. I was so worried. I'm sorry about the wedding."

"It's still on," Sara replied. "At the same place, in my *mamm*'s garden. Just with a different theme."

"Wet Wedding?" Albert asked, frowning. "I can't see it happening."

"You don't have faith," Alicia said. "I can see a wedding happening because they want to be married. And we'll pitch in and help."

"We will?" Albert asked, wincing, one eye on the line out the door.

"We will." Alicia the Awesome stared down her ornery husband.

Albert finally smiled. "If you two are willing to help us out today, I will bring my barrel-cookers to your mom's yard tomorrow and we'll have us some barbecue along with whatever dainty stuff you have planned."

Abram grinned. "That is a deal, *mei* friend. I like that as much as I...like dainty stuff."

Alicia took Sara by her arm while Albert explained the chores Abram could do.

"Sara," Alicia said, "if you still want to work here for a while after you're married, I'll give you a raise and Albert the Alligator will be glad to have you."

"That's so kind," Sara said, Lilah there listening while the men talked about barbecue. "But why?"

Alicia pushed at her frazzled ponytail. "Remember the day you gave that man a doughnut and Albert got all huffy?"

Sara nodded. "I thought he'd fire me."

"Well, that man came back with several co-workers and they ordered food for a whole crew. He told us he'd left his wallet at home, so he only had pocket change for one doughnut and his wife loves our homemade doughnuts, so he bought her the doughnut. But you gave him one for free. He thought that was so kind and turns out he works as a maintenance person along the road—mowing and planting and clearing. He told his buddies about us. We made more money the day they came in than just about any day since we first opened."

Lilah smiled at her daughter. "That is so special, Sara."

Sara seemed speechless. "I'm glad to hear that. But...how did you know my nickname for him?"

Alicia giggled. "I heard you talking to Abram one day. Laughed my head off and loved it. I teased him about it but he thinks I came up with it. We'll keep it that way."

"I don't know what to say," Sara replied. "But we need to get to work, ain't so?"

Alicia looked at the crowd gathering. "Yes, ma'am."

Then she packed up some sandwiches for

Lilah to take home. "We'll see you tomorrow," she said. "And if you need anything else, let us know."

Lilah and the girls got in the golf cart with Noah. "I'll drive," she said. "You need to rest this afternoon."

"I have one thing to do before I can rest," he told her. "Drive yourselves to the house and I'll use the cart and go take care of it."

"Are you sure you feel up to that?"

"It won't take long," he said. "When I get finished, I'll help with the wedding preparations."

Lilah didn't argue with him. Stubborn, but determined and still looking pale with pain after they'd reached her house, he took off toward the street.

"What is he up to now?" she said as she ushered the girls into the house.

"Maybe he has a wedding surprise," Carol said.

"Always with the surprises around here," Lilah replied, shaking her head. "We have a lot to do, so let's get started in the house and then we'll work on the yard."

"I can find vases and pots for the flowers," Dana offered. "After we tidy in here."

"I'll help," Carol said. "Mamm, can I change clothes?"

Lilah realized they'd all slept in damp clothes.

"We should all freshen up while we have the house to ourselves," she said.

She wanted to look decent before Noah returned. She had hastily grabbed a *kapp* after Sara and Abram had shown up.

After the girls went off to change, she stopped and looked out at the gazebo. "Before Noah returns," she whispered. "That had a nice ring to it."

But she still wanted to know what had happened between yesterday and today, besides a massive storm hitting them, of course. Sara seemed like a new person and Noah, even battered and bruised, seemed mighty happy. Abram beamed like a lighthouse flashing. They'd all obviously had a better night than she had.

"They must have had one very interesting talk," she decided. Something she'd never imagined happening.

Just like she'd never imagined her daughter wanting to get married in a wet, torn-apart garden. Something had shifted along with the wind and rain last night, something that had settled her moody daughter and brought Lilah and Noah back together.

Had Noah wanted to come and explain himself?

She'd get her answers from one of them, somehow. For now, she'd enjoy the quiet and pray this wedding went off without any more problems. When she glanced back out the window, she saw a rainbow lifting out through the remaining clouds.

"*Gott*'s will," she told herself. Then she hummed as she washed up, put on a clean cotton dress and a matching *kapp* and got on with her day as if her world had not been turned topsy-turvy.

Chapter Twenty-One

Noah had searched everywhere for the foot-wide brass butterfly finial that had been blown off the gazebo by the storm. The finial was fairly heavy, but in his haste, he might not have tightened it enough for it to stay atop the dome of the structure. But where could it have gone?

He'd driven around and around, taking the way the wind had blown into consideration as he checked rubble piles and asked people if they'd seen the finial. Butterfly finials were pretty common, but this one had been special, vintage and over a century old. He'd paid extra for it, but that wasn't the point. He wanted something special for Lilah and this design really stood out from the rest.

What if he never found it? He could buy another one, but the gazebo wouldn't be the same. He needed to find the one he'd known would be perfect. A swallowtail—bronze with etched black in the wings. One of a kind, the antique dealer had told him.

Just like Lilah.

He rounded a curb, deciding he needed to head back and return this cart to its owner. He'd asked a lot of people about the decorative topper so maybe someone would alert him about it.

He made it back to the house of the man who owned the golf cart. Parking it on the street near some limbs and trash, Noah turned and stood up, but he became dizzy.

"Hey, mister, are you okay?"

He heard the voice from far away. Trying to steady himself, he blinked but everything starting spinning like a top.

"Somebody help us," the young man said. "Send that EMT over this way."

"I'll be okay," Noah said. "Just need to find—"

He fought against the darkness, but it overtook him anyway.

He heard voices, felt people touching his face, head and neck. "He's injured but someone has doctored him," another voice called out. "Let's get him to the church."

In his head, Noah screamed, "I don't need to go to church. I need to get back to Lilah." Would he ever find the time to tell her he loved her?

* * *

Lilah checked the clock. "It's getting late. I'm worried about Noah."

Abram glanced up from sawing limbs. He and Sara had returned home after the café ran out of food, and he'd gone straight to work on cutting up wood and placing it in a pile on the far side of the yard, out of sight. "How long has he been gone?"

"Over an hour or so," she said. "I didn't want him to leave, but he said he had something to do."

She put down her broom and stretched, her gaze moving over the yard. It looked better already, but the girls had insisted on keeping some of the fallen blossoms they gathered. They'd dropped them along the paths she'd built into the garden. So they only worked on picking up broken branches or damaged petals. Carol and Sara had gathered several vases and filled them with hibiscus and roses and taken some old bowls and floated magnolias and gardenias in them. They were lined up on the porch until they could be moved to tables tomorrow.

Lilah wanted to place some of the blossoms and fronds they'd saved around the gazebo.

Staring up at it, her heart stopped. "The butterfly, Abram."

Her soon-to-be son-in-law looked confused. “What butterfly?”

“The one that topped the gazebo. It got knocked off during the storm and Noah said he’d take care of it. What if he went to look for it?”

“In this mess?” Abram glanced about. “And in his condition?”

“He wouldn’t listen to me,” she said. “We need to find him.”

Abram pulled out his work phone. “I’ll call him.”

She waited, thinking she shouldn’t be going through this again. This worrying all the time about a man. She’d been through that once. Her heart couldn’t take this tug and pull, not after last night and how close they’d all come to being swept away. Especially Noah.

Noah was being reckless. She wasn’t used to that and even though he’d been so brave and thoughtful in coming to check on her, she’d feared he’d really injured himself.

“He’s not answering,” Abram said. “I’ll go drive around. He might be helping someone.”

“Or he might be somewhere hurting,” she replied. “He needs to be checked by a doctor.”

“If I find him, I’ll see to that,” Abram assured her.

“I don’t need a butterfly, Abram. I need Noah

to get back here and tell me what he couldn't tell me earlier. You all know—you and Noah and Sara. I need to know, too, before I let things go any further with him."

Sara walked up after seeing Abram on his phone. "Mamm, let's go sit for a while and I'll explain why Abram and I went to see Noah last night."

Lilah studied Sara's face and saw nothing but an earnest need to talk. "All right. I could use some of that lemonade you brought home."

"How about one of Albert the Alligator's chocolate croissants to go with it? Alicia saved us a couple."

"That would be nice," Lilah said. But she didn't think she'd be able to eat a bite.

Noah woke with a jerk, his head foggy with leftover dreams and unfinished business. "Where am I?"

"You're in a makeshift clinic in the church meeting room," a young *Englisch* man explained to Noah. "You passed out on the street. You have a slight concussion and a cracked rib."

"I know all of that," Noah said, trying to sit up. "I have to get back…to my family."

The young man pushed him back down with a gentle hand. "Just rest for a minute. I'm Doctor Kenneth Connor. If you can give me your name, I'll check the missing list."

A missing list. "I'm not missing—I just got dizzy. I'm Noah Lantz, and I need to go."

"Noah Lantz?" The doctor chuckled. "You built my grandparents' Florida retirement home. The cutest little beach cottage. That's why I'm here. They let me use it for a week's vacation and then a hurricane comes."

"Did the home survive?" Noah had to ask.

"It did, sir. A few branches hit the roof and I might need that checked, but the house is intact. My grandparents told me it was solid."

"I'm glad they like it and that it's solid, *sohn*," Noah replied, touched but impatient. "But I came through the storm last night to tell a woman I loved her and I still haven't been able to do that. Can you help me?"

"After I check you over," Dr. Connor said with a smile. "I think you're mostly dehydrated but you need to watch that concussion. Like I said, it's mild but you need to rest. If you promise to follow my directions and then follow up with the doctors at the medical center on Monday, I'll drive you anywhere you want. My shift here is ending in ten minutes."

"Deal," Noah said. "And hey, you haven't seen a brass butterfly about this wide and this high, have you?" He extended his hands to show the size.

"No butterflies that large in here today, Mr. Lantz. Are you sure you're not hallucinating?"

Noah rolled his eyes. "It came off a gazebo I just finished building."

"I see," the young doctor said, grinning. "Does that gazebo have anything to do with this woman you're in love with?"

"Everything, *sohn*, everything," Noah said. "Let's go."

"I have to meet her," the doctor said. "If you got out in that storm to find her, she must be very important to you."

"That she is."

He checked Noah's vitals, which seemed to take forever, then held a penlight to his eyes. After asking Noah what day it was and other significant questions, the doctor scribbled a prescription for pain.

"I'm going to release you only because I'm afraid you'll walk right out of here anyway. But if you don't show up at the big clinic Monday morning, I'll come and find you."

"You have my word," Noah replied. "Now can you get me to Lilah?"

"Give me five more minutes to wash up."

Noah waited, studying the people around him on cots, most of them banged-up like him.

Grateful that he'd been taken care of, he sat still, checking himself for dizziness. He sipped his water and waited. He did not want to pass out again.

But he would find that butterfly ornament, somehow. And he'd find Lilah and tell her how much he wanted to spend the rest of his life with her.

"So what is the big secret?" Lilah asked Sara. They were on the front porch. Carol and Dana were inside making peanut butter and jelly sandwiches.

Sara took her cup of lemonade and sat down in the other rocking chair. "I had to talk to Noah, Mamm."

"I thought as much, but what did you need to see him about?"

Sara took a sip of water. "You."

"Me." It wasn't a question. Lilah waited for the rest.

"I was so wrong, trying to keep you and Noah apart and once I told Abram why, he said I had to make it right."

"You're scaring me, Sara," Lilah said. "Just tell me the truth, please."

"I will but let me get it all out before you get upset," Sara said, a plea in her words.

"I won't say a word."

Lilah sat and listened to Sara pour out her heart—a promise to her dying father. A promise that she'd find something beautiful to put in the yard. But in holding to that promise, she'd brought another man into her mother's life.

"So that's why you fought against Noah and were all wishy-washy about all of this?"

"*Ja*," Sara said, her voice cracking. "I'm so sorry. I see it now. Daed planted that seed in my head and I think he was trying to tell me it would be okay if someone else helped you finish your garden. But I couldn't see that at first."

Sara wiped her eyes and took Lilah's hand. "I like Noah so much, but I loved my *daed*. It was too much, seeing you with someone else and being happy."

Lilah reached for her daughter. They both stood and she wrapped her arms around her daughter. "Oh, Sara, *mei liebling*, what a burden you have carried. You did this for me because of something your *daed* said, which is one of the sweetest gestures on his part and yours. But you know he wants all of us to be happy and to live life. I can see that now, and I hope you do, too."

"I can, Mamm. Daed did want you to continue your life, with the garden, and with someone to love you. You are so lovable and Noah needs you."

Lilah laughed through her tears. "So are you, Sara. I only wish you'd told me this long ago."

"Daed didn't want me to tell you. He only wanted me to make something special happen in your garden."

"Well, that something special is your wedding, not that gazebo."

"But now, we have both, ain't so? The gazebo is standing. The grass withereth, the flower fadeth—"

"—But the word of our God shall stand forever," Lilah replied. "Sara, you continue to amaze me."

"I want you to be as happy as I am. I want you to get to know Noah and hopefully, there will be another wedding by this gazebo one day."

"First, we have to find Noah," Lilah said. "And when we do, I'll tell him you explained everything. Right after I give him a *gut* piece of my mind for leaving while he is injured."

Sara giggled. "You two are perfect for each other."

Chapter Twenty-Two

Abram came back about an hour later. And Noah was with him.

"Noah." Lilah was washing mud off one of the benches. She tried not to run through the yard, but her feet moved with swift action toward Noah. He had new bandages on his cuts, and he had on clean clothes. "Where were you?"

"I found him at the church," Abram explained. "A triage clinic had been set up there. He passed out nearby, but someone got him help."

"Were you looking for the butterfly?" she asked, anger mixed with relief.

"I was," Noah said. "But I couldn't find it—yet."

Lilah didn't know whether to hug him or fuss at him. "I don't need some fancy ornament on the gazebo, Noah. It is fine and you need to rest."

"We took a cab to his house," Abram said. "I thought he was going to sleep but he told the cab to wait. Then he cleaned up and changed so he could get back here."

"I'm better. My rib is just bruised and I have pain pills. I need to move my truck and I wanted to help out." Noah lowered his head. "And I really want to talk to you alone, Lilah."

Lilah glanced at Abram. "I would like that. Sara and I have discussed a lot of things today, you being one of them."

Abram took the hint. "I'm gonna…uh…go find something to do on the other side of the yard. My parents are bringing over some fried chicken later."

Lilah nodded and Noah waved Abram away. "That's nice to hear."

Abram took off in a hurry. That left them standing by the gazebo.

"So you know now," Noah said, his gaze holding her, searching her face. "I'm sorry, Lilah."

"You did nothing wrong," she said as they walked up into the still wet gazebo. "I'm sorry for what I said. I was so torn between wanting to see you and wanting to honor my husband. It's been difficult, and you can't keep doing all those reckless things, Noah. I lost one man. I can't deal with you not using the brain *Gott* gave you."

Noah's lips twitched, and he put a hand over his mouth.

"You think this is humorous?"

"I think I love you," he said, laughing. "I think I fell for you the moment you ordered me out of your house."

"I can do that again if you don't take care of yourself."

"I'll have you to take care of me, won't I?"

She gave him one last frown, then tears started rolling down her face. "*Ja*, you will have me and *ja*, I will take care of you."

"And we have Sara's blessings?"

"We do. The poor confused girl. She is strong, she keeps her promises. And she has promised me that she wants us to be together."

"Can I hug you?"

Lilah glanced around, then smiled. "I'd love that."

Noah pulled her into his arms there in the gazebo. "I gotta find that butterfly. It's the icing on the cake."

"Only if I go search with you," she said.

Then they heard a squeal and Dana came running from a cluster of crushed palmetto bushes. "Hey, I found something. It's that finished thing you keep talking about, Noah."

"Finished?" He laughed. "You mean the finial."

Dana lifted her hands and shrugged. "*Ja*, the butterfly."

They parted and glanced over at her.

"The butterfly," they said together.

Noah kissed Lilah and hurried toward Dana. "It was right here all along."

"Just like everything else," Lilah replied, thanking *Gott.*

"Just hidden," Dana said, handing the heavy ornament to Noah. "Now you can finish the gazebo."

"And so I will."

He was about to climb up the nearby ladder, but Lilah stopped him. "Abram will do it."

Noah grinned. "*Ja*, he will."

Noah gave Abram instructions and the tools he'd need. "Get the butterfly on there *gut* and firm, Abram."

Abram scrambled up the ladder with the finial in one hand. Noah and Lilah sent Dana up the ladder to pass tools to Abram.

In no time at all, he secured the finial with heavy screws and some strong weatherproof glue. "That ought to hold a long, long time."

Noah helped him down, then looked over at Lilah. "I believe it will."

After Abram took the ladder back to the storage shed, Noah put his hand in Lilah's. "Are you sure?"

"I am," she said. "There is no rush. We need

to truly get to know each other, but you know me so well already."

"I think I do," he said as they walked slowly through the blossoms all over the yard. "You can cook. You love butterflies. You love to garden. You can be bossy and ornery, but in a cute way, and you're beautiful. I love you and I love your girls."

"And I know you're a hard worker who uses the best materials to build houses the Amish way—to last. You would do anything for anyone, including going out during a hurricane. You're not fancy, Noah. And I love that about you."

"So you love me?"

"Didn't I say that?"

"Not straight-out."

She grabbed him by his suspenders and held him close. "I love you, Noah. Now how much do I owe you for the gazebo?"

"How about spending the rest of your life with me?"

"You drive a hard bargain," she said. "Done."

The next morning, the family gathered in the yard with the bishop and ministers for the wedding of Sara Mehl and Abram Troyer. The food had been warmed by the propane stoves up and down the street and now sat ready to eat on a long table on the porch, with more inside the kitchen. Several tables covered with white cloths were set out under the damp trees, surrounded by the blossom-covered grass. Vases full of fragrant flowers were centered on each table and all around the gazebo. The brass swallowtail butterfly finial shone bright in the morning sunlight.

Lilah and the girls wore light mint dresses with crisp white aprons and Sara's attendants wore their flamingo pink dresses with newly sewn white linen *kapps*. Sara wore a pale creamy yellow dress and carried a bouquet of mixed flowers from the garden, a gift from her sisters.

They were preparing last-minute things before they'd start the ceremony when other people began to come in through the gate, carrying food and gifts. Then Albert the Alligator had two burly men rolling in two massive barrel-cookers to be placed on the far side of the yard, out of the way. He quietly fired them up and threw chicken, steak and pork onto the sizzling grills, his wife Alicia right by his side. Ramona brought in an oversize white cake with a huge pink sugary hibiscus centered on the top.

Then more people came, with more food.

"I can't believe this," Sara said, watching as the men marched into place, followed by women and children. "Did we invite all of these people?"

"We didn't," Lilah said, "but Martha, Ramona and I put out the word that we'd have plenty of food and we needed to get rid of it quickly. I think the whole of Pinecraft is coming to your wedding, Sara."

Her daughter smiled and watched as the yard filled with *Englisch*, Amish, Mennonites, tourists and snowbirds.

"Amazing," Carol said, clapping her hands. "The best wedding ever."

"And with so many unexpected things bringing us all together," Lilah replied.

"Does that include Noah?" Sara asked as they watched from the kitchen window.

"He was the most unexpected part of all of this," Lilah replied. "I got a suitor along with my gazebo. A *gut* bargain."

As if he knew she was watching him, Noah glanced up and waved to her. She waved back. "Let's go get you married, Sara. I do believe my garden is finally finished."

"But new flowers and new crops will return," Dana said.

"Always," Lilah told her daughters.

Later, as she listened to the ministers and watched as Sara and Abram sat up front patiently listening, too, she glanced over and saw Noah. He gave her a smile that lit up her heart.

Denke, Joshua, she thought. And *denke*, Gott.

Then she looked out over the garden. The battered plants had recovered and the blossoms on the ground sparkled like rare jewels. A swallow-tailed black-and-yellow butterfly lifted off from an orange tree and fluttered away out into the blue sky.

Lilah took that as a *gut* sign with which to begin her new life. Her daughter had kept her promise.

And *Gott* had guided them through yet another storm.

Much later, after everyone had left, Noah found her and pulled her close. "So what's next?"

"Supper," she said. "We have lots of leftovers and the power is back on."

He nodded his approval. "Supper, walks to the park, Sunday ice cream, helping Abram and Sara get settled, helping rebuild the damaged homes and businesses and deciding our future."

"Well, that should keep us busy for the next thirty years at least."

Noah took her hand and they went to sit in the gazebo while the gloaming came in glistening rays of golden sunset over the yard. "I sure hope so," he said. "Meantime..."

Then he kissed her.

* * * * *

Dear Reader,

This book had not been planned, but I had to come up with a new plot quickly and a gazebo popped into my head. From there, I decided I needed a wedding.

So that's how this book got started. I also wanted to write about older characters, so meeting Noah and Lilah was a joy. They were both suffering from grief, which we know can change a person's perspective on life.

That made me think about the storms of life—the real ones that can destroy everything we love and the internal ones that we fight every day while we carry on with a smile on our face. Those internal storms are just as challenging as storms that pass through and leave destruction. I love how Noah and Lilah worked through both and came out together. And I also loved how Sara found her way in the storm, too.

If you're going through your own emotional storm, know that you are not alone. I was fighting those dark clouds and lightning with every word in this book. But I was smiling at the end as I pictured that beautiful gazebo in Lilah's yard.

I hope you did the same when you read the book.

Until next time—may the angels watch over you. Always.

Lenora Worth